The Boy Who Caught The Oceans

Journey of a Dreamer Bound by the Tides

By

Nick Thornton

This is a work of fiction. Similarities to real people, places, or events are entirely coincidental.

THE BOY WHO CAUGHT THE OCEANS

First edition. September 30, 2024.

Copyright © 2024 Nick Thornton.

ISBN: 979-8227567291

Written by Nick Thornton.

Chapter 1

In a quaint little village, a hidden gem nestled snugly along a rugged yet breathtaking coastline, Leo found his home. This enchanting village, effortlessly charming in its character, was adorned with picturesque cobblestone streets that wound their way through a tapestry of colourful cottages. Each cottage was embellished with vibrant flower boxes, overflowing with an array of blossoms that danced in the coastal breeze, their colours showcasing nature's palette. The village, steeped in the rich history that echoed through its very stones, was surrounded by breathtaking vistas—craggy cliffs that jutted into the azure sea, lush green hills that rolled gently into the distance, and a horizon that seemed to go on forever.

As he inhaled the crisp, salty sea air, Leo savoured the mingling scents of fresh lavender and wild thyme, fragrant reminders of the untamed beauty surrounding him. An exhilarating breeze swept through the area, carrying whispers of the ocean and filling the air with a refreshing vitality. Each day, the wind would weave its way through the gnarled branches of ancient oaks that stood sentinel along the pathways, their roots buried deep in the earth, a testament to the countless seasons they had weathered. The trees seemed to hold secrets, timeless stories of joy and sorrow that had unfolded in their shade, and they shared these tales in hushed tones, inviting the attentive ear of anyone who cared to listen.

The ocean itself was alive, its waves performing a rhythmic dance as they crashed against the rocky shores with a powerful yet soothing force. Each surge sent plumes of frothy white spray cascading into the air, sparkling like diamonds in the warm sunlight. The shoreline was a playground for the village children, who ran along the water's edge, their laughter harmonizing beautifully with the sounds of the waves. Boats bobbed gently in the bustling harbour, their bright colours reflecting on the water's surface, creating a lively scene that pulsed with life. Fishermen, guided by the wisdom passed down through generations, adeptly learned the craft from fathers and grandfathers before them. They spun tales of grand adventures and the mysteries lurking beneath the waves, captivating anyone within earshot, their stories woven into the very fabric of village lore.

However, amidst this idyllic setting, Leo is not like the other children. While they revelled in the simple joys of village life—playing games on the sandy shore, building castles, and exploring the hidden nooks and crannies of their surroundings—Leo harboured a secret that set him apart from his peers. Beneath his joyful exterior, he possessed a magical ability that filled him with both wonder and confusion. While he shared their innocent mischief and exuberant spirit, there was an additional layer to Leo, an innate gift that connected him to the very essence of nature.

Leo's extraordinary talent allowed him to communicate with the elements in a way that few could comprehend. The ocean's tides would respond to his emotions, rising and falling as if they were an extension of his own thoughts and feelings. When he laughed, the winds seemed to carry that laughter far and wide, echoing across the hills and through the village. Flowers, too, would bloom with a vibrancy unmatched by any other, unfurling their petals in joyful salute whenever Leo was near. The trees, wise and ancient, would bend their branches gently towards him, as if eager to impart their timeless wisdom, connecting with the young boy who bore such a unique bond with the natural world.

In the quiet moments by the shore, where the rhythm of the waves provided a soothing backdrop, Leo often found solace. These were times when he could freely confess his feelings to the vast, eternal ocean, exploring the depths of his powers in a sanctuary of serenity. Yet, beneath this enchantment lay a sense of understanding that, while his gift was special, it also separated him from the others. With a heavy heart, he watched as the village children forged deeper connections, their bonds strengthened through shared experiences and whispered secrets, while he remained an enigma—mysterious and distant, shrouded by the aura of his unique abilities.

Secretly, amidst the longing and isolation, Leo nurtured dreams of a brighter future. He envisioned a way to bridge the gap between himself and the other villagers, to share his magic with them, to reveal the breathtaking beauty that unfolded before his eyes—a beauty only he could perceive. The endless possibilities of his powers felt both thrilling and daunting, igniting a fire of ambition within him. Leo understood that the time would come, inevitably, when he would have to embrace who he truly was—a boy destined for extraordinary adventures that awaited him just beyond the horizon, in a world where the breath of nature and the whispers of the ocean beckoned him forth into the unknown.

Leo could catch the oceans in his hands, a magical ability that set him apart in ways he never could have imagined. It was a peculiar gift, one that he discovered quite by accident during a sun-drenched afternoon at the beach, a place that would become his favoured retreat far beyond his toddler years. The salty breeze danced around him playfully as he toddled down the sandy stretch, his little legs moving with an excited determination. The air was warm and fragrant, infused with the scent of salt and freedom, a perfect backdrop for the adventures that awaited him.

With wide, curious eyes reflecting the shimmering blue of the waves, he stood at the shoreline, captivated by the rhythmic ebb and flow of the water. Each crash of the waves seemed to sing a song that only he could hear, a melody woven from the whispers of the sea and the laughter of the wind, inviting him closer to the edge where land met the sea. Leo's heart raced with thrill and wonder as he took careful steps, his feet sinking into the cool, wet sand that moulded around him like a welcoming embrace.

As he reached out, his tiny fingers brushed against the foamy crests, leaving small trails in the wet sand. The sensation was exhilarating; the water felt alive, breathing and pulsing against his skin. Leo giggled, letting out childish squeals of delight as he playfully splashed at the shore, marvelling at how the foam danced around his tiny hands as if it were celebrating his presence.

To his utter surprise, the water inexplicably responded to his touch. Instead of receding into the vast ocean, it seemed to pause, hesitating for a moment as if feeling a strange connection to him—a bond that neither he nor the waves fully understood. It was as if the sea recognized him, a kindred spirit in this endless expanse of blue. With every gentle wave that lapped at his feet, Leo felt as though the ocean was inviting him deeper into its embrace, promising adventures and secrets hidden just beneath the surface.

It wasn't just that the water clung to him; it was as though it yearned to be held, willingly pooling in his palms and forming droplets that sparkled like diamonds in the sunlight. Each drop felt heavy with stories of distant shores and hidden treasures, waiting patiently to be shared with the young boy who possessed such a remarkable gift. Leo marvelled at the magic he held, his palms cradling the essence of the ocean as he giggled in sheer delight.

The sun dipped lower in the sky, casting a golden hue across the landscape, and turning the ocean into a canvas of shifting colours. The waves continued their dance, rising and falling in perfect harmony, and Leo felt a surge of joy and contentment. He was not merely a child playing by the sea; he was a keeper of the ocean's secrets, a young guardian who had uncovered a connection that would bind him to this magical place for years to come.

From that moment on, every visit to the beach promised new discoveries and countless memories, as Leo embraced his extraordinary ability to catch the oceans in his hands, forever drawn to the spellbinding dance between the land and the sea. Little did he know, this wondrous gift would soon lead him on a journey far beyond the gently lapping waves and sandy shores, into a world where magic, adventure, and destiny awaited.

In that moment of innocent wonder, Leo found himself entranced, his laughter mingling joyfully with the rhythmic sound of the surf crashing against the shore. It was a day when the sun shone brightly, painting the sky in myriad shades of blue, and the salty breeze danced around him like a playful companion. What had initially seemed like an ordinary day at the beach, filled with the familiar sights of sunbathers, children building castles in the sand, and seagulls swooping overhead, quickly transformed into a fantastical discovery that would alter the course of his life. As he frolicked in the shallows, a peculiar glimmer beneath the surface caught his eye—a gift from the ocean, mysterious and alluring, pulled him into a world brimming with possibility. That extraordinary moment, when he realized he could harness the ocean's depths with just a simple touch, ignited a spark in him, filling him with an exhilarating mix of excitement and an unshakeable sense of responsibility.

As the years passed and Leo grew older, he found himself drawn back to the shoreline time and time again, with his heart brimming with anticipation and a myriad of unanswered questions swirling in his mind. Each visit became a ritual, a sacred opportunity to delve into the vast depths of his extraordinary gift. With each encounter, he learned the nuances of his power—how to beckon the waves to rise high, crashing dramatically against the rocks, and how to gently calm the tides to create a serene oasis. He discovered the joy of summoning small puddles of water that danced at his fingertips and of dispersing the ocean into playful sprays that glistened like diamonds in the sun.

However, with every new skill he mastered, the weight of his power also grew heavier on his young shoulders. He often found himself pondering the deeper implications of such a profound connection with nature. What were the responsibilities that came with such incredible abilities? Should he share his secret with others, or would the knowledge of his powers invite danger and greed? These questions swirled around in his head like the tides he commanded, each wave revealing more of the ocean's mysteries while simultaneously deepening his understanding of the delicate balance between humanity and nature.

Little did he know, that this unique ability to bend the waters would lead him on a journey beyond his wildest dreams. It would bring him friendships with those who shared his passion for the sea, introduce him to mentors who would guide him in understanding his powers, and present challenges that would test his character and resolve. As he navigated the complexities of his life, the ocean would whisper its secrets—tales of forgotten shipwrecks, ancient legends, and treasures hidden beneath the waves—waiting to be uncovered by a boy who dared to dream, a boy who would grow into a guardian of the sea and its boundless wonders.

As the years passed and Leo continued to mature, his remarkable ability to control water deepened and evolved in ways that astonished those around him. No longer just a child playing with the ocean's waves, Leo found himself mastering this extraordinary gift, as if it were an extension of his very being, intertwined with his identity. With effortless grace, he would cup his hands together and scoop up a handful of seawater, raising it high above his head like a precious gem that caught the light. It sparkled and glittered in the sunlight, dancing playfully in the air before cascading back down in a shimmering waterfall, a reflection of the wild beauty of the sea.

His connection with water was profoundly unique; it offered him a conduit of communication with the natural world. This bond allowed him to manipulate the fluid element with an uncanny precision that left his friends and family often speechless. With the simple flick of his wrist or focused thought, he could mould and shape the liquid into strange and wondrous forms, bending it to his will with elegant ease. In the comforting privacy of his home, he would transform mundane routines into magical experiences; take his bathtub, for example. In that small, confined space, he'd conjure miniature tidal waves that surged and crashed against the porcelain sides, echoing the grandeur and fierce power of the ocean. The water would foam and bubble, creating an atmosphere filled with adventure and delight, fooling his senses into believing he was riding the waves of a vast ocean instead of simply splashing in a tub.

Leo revelled in the beauty of creation, particularly during those afternoons spent by the sea or in the comfort of his home. Every droplet of water that clung to his skin after a long day in the ocean became a canvas for his imagination. He would meticulously craft intricate sculptures from these droplets, creating delicate formations that appeared to shimmer with life. These translucent creations could take on the shapes of fantastical creatures that swam through his dreams, towering castles that felt like they were plucked right from the pages of a storybook, or even fierce deep-sea monsters that brought forth an element of thrill and fear. Each piece was more elaborate than the last, intricately detailed and steeped in the essence of a world both real and imagined.

As word of his extraordinary ability spread, friends and family began to gather around him, drawn in by the magnetic pull of his artistry. They watched in awe as the water responded to his every whim, swirling gracefully around him, taking on life and form, mirroring the creative energy within him. Laughter and gasps of wonder filled the air, an audience entranced by the spectacle. Every formation told a story—each sculpture was not merely water, but a window into the depths of his imagination and the connections he forged with the world around him. With each enchanting display, Leo became not just a creator but a magician in the eyes of those who witnessed his remarkable displays, as he effortlessly bridged the gap between reality and the fantastical possibilities that flowed through him like the tides of the ocean.

In every droplet of water, Leo discovered a vast universe of opportunities, a profound reflection of his inner self that held the power to both enchant and inspire all who were fortunate enough to witness his extraordinary gift. With each splash and ripple, he found a silent connection to something greater than himself. The way the sunlight danced on the surface of the water became a canvas for his fantasies, and the whispers of the waves called to his adventurous spirit. As he wholeheartedly embraced his abilities, his imagination blossomed like a vibrant flower reaching for the sky, unfurling its petals to allow the bright light of creativity to pour in. He began to envision a series of limitless adventures, journeys woven with threads of courage and curiosity, where water became not just a companion but a loyal ally. Each escapade promised to unveil the depths of his true potential while revealing the enchanting bond that flowed between nature and his very essence.

His parents, though initially taken aback by the astonishing connection their son had with the ocean, slowly transitioned from bewilderment to acceptance, allowing themselves to fully appreciate Leo's extraordinary talent. In the beginning, they felt a mixture of confusion and concern as they grappled with the implications of his unusual affinity for the sea. The vastness of it all loomed large, and they were uncertain about how to support him in navigating this new reality that had seemingly upended their lives. However, as time wore on and Leo's passion flourished, they began to see not only the beauty but the profound significance of his gift. They decided against stifling his spirit or pushing him towards more conventional paths, instead choosing to encourage him to explore the depths of his abilities in their entirety. Their hearts swelled with pride as they urged him to dive into the mysteries of the ocean—both literally, through his adventurous swims, and metaphorically, through the vast uncharted waters of his imagination.

To nurture his swirling curiosity, they filled their home with tales of wonder from their own childhoods, crafting a tapestry of enchanting stories laced with the magic of ancient civilizations and forgotten folklore. They transported him to realms where mermaids with their iridescent tails glided gracefully through crystal-clear waters, their melodic voices weaving songs that could charm even the weariest of sailors into surrendering to the gentle pull of the tides. They shared legends of mighty sea gods, powerful entities who were believed to command the tides and storms, their tempers fierce enough to tame even the most dauntless of ships. Leo listened with rapt attention, his sparkling eyes wide with awe, and as he absorbed each story, his imagination took flight, soaring into the depths of new possibilities. Each tale ignited a vivid vision within him, painting elaborate pictures of the underwater realm, a magical world where he could lose himself in the extraordinary adventures that awaited him beneath the waves. The ocean, with its endless mysteries, became his muse, and he was eager to dive into the depths of it all, both inspiring and shaping the boy he was destined to become.

The enchanting tales of the ocean's profound mysteries and captivating creatures became a wellspring of inspiration for Leo, igniting a fire of creativity within him that was unlike anything he had ever experienced. It wasn't merely the stories that enthralled him; it was the profound yearning that awakened in him—a desire to delve deeper into the ocean's secrets, to unveil the rich tapestry of life that lay beneath the waves. As he listened to his parents recount these legends, Leo's imagination soared to new heights, painting vivid pictures in his mind of majestic beings gliding gracefully through the water. He often found himself envisioning swimming alongside these mythical creatures, weaving through intricate coral reefs pulsating with vibrant colours and bustling with life. With each swirling current and flickering fish, he imagined forging a connection with the very elements that had captured his heart since he was a child.

Each story shared at the dinner table or during tranquil evenings by the shore, filled Leo with an insatiable curiosity and a resolute commitment to uncover the hidden truths that the ocean had held tightly for centuries. The more his parents embraced his fascination and encouraged his explorations into marine lore, the stronger his resolve grew. It was as if they were embarking on this journey together, their mutual love for the ocean creating an unbreakable bond that united them through threads of imagination and explorative adventure. Each shared discovery and new learning about the marine world acted as a glue, drawing them closer and nurturing a familial spirit intertwined with the rich history of the sea.

However, amid this blooming passion for the ocean, Leo found himself grappling with a deep-seated loneliness that echoed around him like an empty hull. His extraordinary gift—one that set him apart from his peers—was a double-edged sword. While some were undeniably fascinated, the stark reality remained that most of the children in the village viewed his unique talent with suspicion, misunderstanding, and even outright fear. For them, Leo's abilities were strange, provoking reactions that often turned harsh. Instead of nurturing their curiosity and engaging with him, the village kids chose to mock and ridicule Leo. They would laugh cruelly, showering him with taunts every time they saw him channelling his gift, seemingly oblivious to the beauty within his unusual skill. Their laughter pierced through his heart, turning what should have been joyous expressions of creativity and connection into experiences of profound isolation and heartache, each jeer deepening the chasm between him and his peers.

In moments of despair, when the weight of his isolation grew unbearable and the taunts soured the little joy he could muster, Leo sought refuge at the beach. This secluded sanctuary, with its soft, warm sand beneath his feet and the briny scent of the sea air swirling around him, offered solace as nothing else could. Here, the vast and endless ocean stretched out before him—a boundless expanse that seemingly mirrored the depths of his sorrow and longing. The rhythmic crash of the waves against the shore played a gentle, soothing symphony, providing a perfect backdrop for his tumultuous thoughts, a melody that enveloped him as if in a warm embrace.

Standing at the water's edge, Leo would close his eyes, allowing himself to be swept away by the symphony of the surf. In those precious moments, he experienced an unparalleled sense of belonging—a feeling that the sea understood him in profound ways that none of the other children ever could. Each crashing wave felt like a friend reaching out to him, extending a warm welcome and resonating with the whirlwind of emotions he often struggled to articulate. The ocean was more than just a backdrop to his solitude; it was a living, breathing entity that reflected his innermost thoughts and feelings. Like a companion who listened without judgment, it offered him solace, inspiration, and an understanding he yearned for, transforming his moments of isolation into opportunities for self-discovery and creative expression. Every interaction with the sea deepened his resolve to pursue the mysteries of marine life, igniting a lifelong passion that would ultimately shape who he was meant to become.

With every burst of foam and spray of saltwater, Leo felt himself becoming part of something larger than himself, an intricate web of life that pulsed and throbbed with energy all around him. He would often find a secluded spot on the beach, sitting for hours in serene solitude, collecting seashells of every conceivable shape and hue, marvelling at the intricate designs crafted by nature itself. As gulls soared overhead, their calls blending with the rhythmic crash of the waves, the gentle breeze ruffled his hair and swept through his spirit, carrying away the weight of his worries, leaving him lighter, freer. In this harmonious embrace of the ocean, he discovered a profound sense of peace and understanding that often eluded him on land—a bond with nature that transcended the limitations of language, allowing him to connect deeply while overlooking the differences that so often divided people.

Despite the loneliness that occasionally wrapped around his heart like a thick fog, the beach remained a steadfast pillar of strength. It was a constant sanctuary, a place where Leo could retreat to gather his thoughts and re-centre himself. In the secret chambers of his heart, he held onto a flickering hope, a vision of a future where he might meet someone who could truly appreciate his unique gifts and see the beauty that lay within him. He dreamed of finding a kindred spirit, someone who shared in his fascination with the world's wonders and the myriad mysteries it held. Yet until that day came, he took solace in knowing that the ocean would always remain his closest companion—a refuge where he could voice his thoughts to the wind, be genuinely himself, free from judgment, and breathe in the exhilarating possibilities that the unknown had to offer.

One enchanting day, while meandering through the rocky coastline, Leo stumbled upon a hidden cove that seemed like a portal to another realm entirely. As he pushed through a thicket of wildflowers and dense bushes, he felt an exhilarating sense of discovery, finally emerging onto a stretch of land that took his breath away, leaving him awestruck. The cove unfolded before him like a breathtaking tableau, a masterpiece painted by nature herself, where the crystal-clear waters sparkled dazzlingly under the brilliant midday sun, reflecting an array of stunning hues—turquoise, aquamarine, and deep sapphire. The sandy beach, soft and warm beneath his bare feet, appeared to stretch endlessly toward the horizon, inviting him to explore its secrets. Rugged cliffs, draped in verdant greenery, embraced this secluded paradise as if nature itself was cradling him in her gentle arms.

As the sun began its slow descent, illuminating the sky with vibrant shades of orange, blush pink, and regal purple, Leo settled onto the fine sand, leaning back to absorb the calming symphony of the gentle waves lapping rhythmically at the shore. Each swell felt like a heartbeat, echoing deep within him, and he couldn't help but feel an overwhelming sense of serenity and belonging wash over him. In that tranquil moment, as the world around him transformed into a kaleidoscope of colours, it felt as if time suspended itself in this magical place, creating a sanctuary that was exclusively his. This hidden cove became Leo's sacred retreat, a cherished refuge away from the relentless bustle of the village, a serene escape where he could connect intimately with both nature and his own soul.

As the years flowed by like the tides, ebbing and flowing, Leo's extraordinary talents did not go unnoticed. Word of his remarkable abilities spread, and his reputation as the "Boy Who Caught the Oceans" began to ripple through the village and beyond, attracting throngs of curious onlookers eager to witness his unique connection with the sea. Villagers flocked to him in droves; some arrived filled with awe and admiration, their eyes sparkling with wonder as they peppered him with questions about the seemingly impossible gift he possessed. Others, however, approached him with a wary eye, allowing their imaginations to weave intricate tales of superstition, apprehension, and fear surrounding his enigmatic bond with the ocean.

Despite the varied reactions swirling around him, Leo remained grounded, his spirit untouched by the sensationalism that often accompanied his name. He felt a deep-rooted connection to the ocean that far surpassed the opinions of others, a profound understanding that this relationship was something sacred, personal, and irreplaceable. With every venture into the depths of the cove—whether he was swimming among vibrant, darting fish, or marveling at the delicate intricacies of the tide pools that burst with life—his appreciation for the ocean blossomed more than ever. Each day spent exploring his remarkable gift infused him with renewed passion and purpose, a quiet yet undeniable knowing that he was destined to ride the waves of adventure ahead, discovering the myriad boundless mysteries of the sea, while humbly embracing his role as its devoted steward.

Chapter 2

One sunny morning, the golden rays of the sun spilt over the horizon, casting a warm, inviting glow across the rocky shoreline and turning the ocean into a breathtaking canvas of shimmering light. The rhythmic sound of the waves crashing against the jagged rocks created a soothing melody, harmonizing with the chirping of seagulls soaring gracefully overhead. Leo, an adventurous and inquisitive boy with a heart full of wanderlust and an unquenchable thirst for discovery, decided that today was the day he would embark on a journey to explore the hidden cove that was whispered about in stories shared among the townspeople. These tales spoke of sparkling waters and vibrant marine life, igniting a spark of excitement within him.

With a sense of purpose, Leo set off down the winding path that meandered through the towering cliffs, flanked by patches of bright green sea grass and clusters of wildflowers swaying gently in the salty breeze. Each step was filled with anticipation, the cool air tinged with the scent of the ocean, invigorating his spirit and fueling his determination to uncover the secrets of the mysterious cove. The salty breeze danced playfully around him, lifting his hair and filling him with an intoxicating excitement that propelled him forward as if nature itself was urging him on.

After what felt like an exhilarating trek, Leo finally arrived at the cove. His eyes widened in amazement as he took in the breathtaking scene before him: the tide had receded, revealing numerous tide pools that sparkled in the sunlight, glistening like hidden jewels scattered across the rocky canvas. Eagerly, Leo rushed from one pool to another, his curiosity piqued by the enchanting life that thrived within each small basin. He marvelled at the brightly coloured starfish that clung tenaciously to the rocks, their vibrant hues vibrant against the dull stone. Translucent jellyfish drifted gracefully through the shallow waters, their ethereal bodies pulsing softly as they glided with the gentle flow of the sea.

Yet, amidst the lively chaos of the tide pools, one particular pool caught Leo's attention; it was unlike any he had encountered before. This pool was smaller than the others he had seen, almost as if it were a secret kept hidden from the world outside. The water within it appeared to be a mysterious, deep inky blue, reminiscent of the night sky, adorned with shimmering stars. It stood in striking contrast to the bright turquoise waters surrounding it as if it was a portal to another realm. Leo felt an indescribable pull toward this pool as if it were beckoning him to uncover its hidden wonders and reveal what lay beneath its tranquil surface.

With a heart full of wonder, Leo knelt beside the pool, his eyes fixed intently on the mesmerizing depths. As he brought his face closer to the water's surface, he noticed something unusual at the very bottom. Nestled among the smooth pebbles and glimmering grains of sand lay a strange, shimmering object that caught the sunlight in a captivating dance. Its luminescence seemed to pulsate softly, as if alive, reflecting the light in a myriad of colours that twirled and swirled on the water's surface. At that moment, Leo's heart raced with curiosity and intrigue. Questions flooded his mind. What could it be? What stories might this mysterious object hold within its graceful form?

With a sense of determination swelling inside him, Leo prepared to immerse himself in the cool, refreshing water of the tide pool. Cautiously, he dipped his fingers into the inviting depths, sending tiny ripples cascading outward that distorted the reflections around him. The sensation was exhilarating, awakening a deep-seated connection to the ocean's mysteries that lay just beneath his fingertips. Steeling himself for what lies ahead, he reached down towards the mysterious object at the bottom of the pool, his heart pounding with a mix of thrill and trepidation. What revelations awaited him in this seemingly ordinary yet extraordinarily captivating place?

To his surprise, as he grasped the object gently, it revealed itself to be a small, crystalline sphere. Its surface gleamed brilliantly, reflecting the gentle light of its surroundings like a tiny sun captured in his palm. The sphere pulsated rhythmically with a soft, ethereal glow that cast delicate patterns on the ground as Leo turned it over, discovering its enchanting texture. The light appeared to breathe with him, ebbing and flowing like the tide, and with each pulse, he felt an exhilarating surge of energy coursing through his veins. It was as if the sphere was alive, a sentient artefact that held the wisdom of ancient seas, whispering long-forgotten secrets into his very soul.

Leo's curiosity intensified as he pondered the possibilities of what this incredible find could mean. What adventures lay ahead of him now that he held something so remarkable in his hands? What magic did this crystalline sphere hold, and how would it change his life from this moment on? As he stood there, entranced by the artefact's beauty, a sense of destiny enveloped him, reminding him that sometimes, the most extraordinary discoveries could be found in the most unexpected places.

They started whispering secrets of the ocean's depths directly into his consciousness, the small, crystalline orb pulsated gently in Leo's palm, as if alive with its own energy. Images of vibrant coral reefs, rich with hues of orange, pink, and purple, danced before his eyes, while shimmering schools of fish swirled in synchrony, their scales glinting like tiny jewels under the sunlit waters. The haunting calls of distant whales reverberated through his mind, echoing ancient songs that spoke of migration, love, and the natural rhythms of life beneath the waves. Each vision was accompanied by a deep sense of the rich history of the marine world, a narrative of ecosystems that had once thrived in a perfect balance, interwoven with the stories of countless creatures that called the ocean their home.

The sensation was overwhelming, a tidal wave of emotions surging through him, igniting a profound sense of wonder and insatiable curiosity within his very soul. It pulled him closer to the unknown mysteries that awaited his exploration beneath the surface—a world so different yet so intimately connected to his own. He couldn't shake the feeling that this small, crystalline orb was not merely a trinket of exquisite beauty, but rather a key, an extraordinary artifact capable of unlocking profound truths hidden beneath the water's surface. These truths lay in wait, patient and beckoning, for someone brave enough to dive into their depths and illuminate the shadows that concealed them.

Leo dedicated countless hours to the intricate study of the mysterious sphere that had inexplicably come into his possession. With each passing moment, he plunged deeper into its mysteries, yearning to unravel the cryptic messages encoded within its translucent form. As he delved deeper into its secrets, he began to uncover tales of hidden currents—majestic pathways that traveled unseen beneath the waves. He envisioned these currents weaving through the vast expanse of the ocean like invisible highways, guiding not only the delicate dance of marine life but also the vessels of seafarers who relied on these hidden channels to navigate the seemingly endless blue.

With each discovery, he pieced together a tapestry of interconnected relationships: the symbiotic bonds between the vibrant coral reefs and the myriad of species they supported; the mysterious migratory patterns of the whales, who traversed great distances in search of food and mates; and the centuries-old stories of sailors who respected and feared the ocean's unpredictable moods. This growing understanding fueled his thirst for knowledge, propelling him onward in his quest to connect with a world that felt both foreign and familiar, igniting within him a burning desire to preserve the ocean's beauty and its enigmatic secrets for generations yet to come. Each revelation felt like a stepping stone leading him closer to the heart of the ocean's most profound mysteries, revealing the timeless connection between humans and the marine realm that so few had the privilege or foresight to acknowledge.

Leo's journey began with a sense of curiosity that drew him to the intriguing legends surrounding the ocean, a realm that had long captivated human imagination. He immersed himself in countless tales and ancient lore, discovering stories of magnificent sea creatures that once inhabited the depths of the water. These legendary beings were not merely figments of folklore; they were colossal entities, described in vivid detail, leaving an indelible mark on the cultural tapestry of coastal communities. While some chose to dismiss these stories as mere myths, they resonated deeply with those who gazed longingly at the horizon, yearning to understand the mysteries that lay beneath the waves.

As he delved deeper into these narratives, Leo learned of creatures whose wisdom surpassed human comprehension. There were whispers of ethereal beings that communicated through the rhythms of the tides, imparting knowledge to those who dared to listen. These majestic entities embodied the very essence of the ocean—mysterious and captivating, yet vulnerable to the fragility of their environment. Conversely, he encountered tales of terrifying leviathans, whose unpredictable nature invoked fear in the hearts of sailors and fishermen alike. Each story painted a complex picture of a world teeming with life, where beauty and danger coexisted in an intricate dance, and Leo found himself increasingly enraptured by this duality.

As his research advanced, Leo stumbled upon tantalizing hints of an even greater force—an enigmatic guardian tasked with protecting the ocean's secrets. This entity, cloaked in mystery, was said to be the sentinel of the deep, ensuring that the delicate balance of life beneath the surface remained intact. Legends spoke of the guardian's fierce determination to shield the knowledge of the ocean from those who sought to harness it for selfish purposes. Leo began to perceive his emerging connection to this vast marine world not as a serendipitous event, but as part of a grander design, intricately woven into the fabric of existence.

With each piece of information he uncovered, the weight of his discoveries became increasingly palpable. The palpable thrill he had once felt morphed into a profound sense of responsibility, one he had never anticipated. The realization that he had been granted access to the ocean's infinite wisdom imbued him with a sense of duty that transcended personal ambition. He saw himself not just as a researcher or an explorer, but as a guardian in his own right—a custodian tasked with the heavy burden of protecting these sacred secrets. He understood that every choice he made could ripple outward, influencing not just his fate but also the fates of countless creatures that thrived within the ocean's expanse.

Emboldened by this realization, Leo resolved to dedicate his life to a mission that combined a thirst for knowledge with an unwavering commitment to conservation. His understanding of the ocean solidified, transforming it into both a key to unlocking ancient wisdom and a vivid reminder of the responsibilities that accompanied his journey. Each dive into the depths became a profound exploration not just of the marine landscape, but of his very self, as he sought to reconcile the allure of discovery with the imperative to protect. Leo knew he was on the brink of a transformative journey—one that would not only shape his destiny but also illuminate the path toward safeguarding the ocean, ensuring that its timeless secrets would endure for generations to come. As he prepared to plunge into the deep blue waters, he felt the weight of the ocean's mysteries calling to him, urging him onward into the exhilarating unknown.

As Leo delved deeper into the ocean's mysteries, he soon found himself enveloped by an ethereal blue light that danced around him like a soft embrace. Curious and determined, he swam toward the source of this captivating glow, only to uncover an exquisite sphere nestled among vibrant corals and shimmering schools of fish. With each movement, he felt an irresistible pull, as if the sphere itself were beckoning him to come closer.

Upon further investigation, Leo discovered that this enigmatic sphere was not merely a fascinating artefact but was intrinsically linked to a powerful underwater city hidden beneath the waves. As he ventured toward the city's entrance, he was awestruck by its grandeur. Towering structures, crafted from iridescent shells and bioluminescent materials, jutted majestically from the seabed, glowing softly in the dim light of the ocean depths.

As Leo swam through the ornate archways adorned with intricate carvings, he soon realized that the city was not just a place of breathtaking beauty; it was the home of a remarkable race of merpeople. These beings, with their shimmering scales and graceful tails, possessed an ethereal elegance. They had lived in harmony with the ocean for millennia, cultivating a profound understanding of its rhythms and secrets.

The merpeople were not simply inhabitants of this world; they were its guardians, entrusted with the vital responsibility of protecting the delicate balance and harmony of the sea. They revered each creature, from the smallest plankton to the largest whales, recognizing their integral roles within the ecosystem. Their society was built upon respect and cooperation, as they thrived by maintaining the health of their underwater environment, practising sustainable fishing, and nurturing the coral reefs that surrounded them.

As Leo interacted with the merpeople, he learned about their ancient customs and deep-rooted connections to the ocean. They shared stories of their ancestors who had communicated with sea creatures, forging alliances that still endure today. The merpeople demonstrated a profound wisdom that resonated with Leo, showing him how to respect the ocean and its treasures, much as they had done for generations.

In this wondrous underwater city, Leo found a community that not only celebrated the beauty of the marine world but also understood the struggles it faced against pollution and climate change. With each passing day, he became more enchanted by their way of life and their commitment to preserving the ocean's wonders.

As Leo's journey continued, he realized that his discovery of the merpeople and their city was not merely an adventure; it was a calling. He felt an undeniable urge to join forces with these guardians of the sea, to become an advocate for the ocean beyond the shore, to help protect the world he had come to love so dearly. And so, with a heart full of hope and a sense of purpose, Leo embraced his new role, vowing to bridge the gap between his world and the enchanting realm of the merpeople. Together, they would work to ensure that the mysteries of the ocean would remain untarnished for generations to come.

The merpeople had been silently observing Leo for an extended period, hidden beneath the shimmering surface of the water, their graceful forms gliding effortlessly through the depths. They recognized in him a rare gift—a unique connection to the ocean that seemed to resonate with the very rhythms of the sea. The intricate patterns of the tides and the songs of the underwater currents called to Leo in a way that felt almost instinctual, and the merpeople sensed that he was more than just an ordinary human; he was destined to play a crucial role in their world, one that had been foretold in the ancient prophecies of the sea.

As Leo continued his explorations of the tide pool, marvelling at the vibrant marine life and the breathtaking beauty of his surroundings, he began to encounter the merpeople more frequently. Their shimmering scales glinted like jewels in the sunlight, and their laughter bubbled like the waves around him. Slowly, a bond began to form between Leo and these enchanting beings. They were not just guardians of the ocean but stewards of a rich culture steeped in traditions that had flourished for centuries beneath the waves.

In their underwater realm, the merpeople eagerly embraced him, eager to share their wisdom. They taught Leo their intricate language, filled with melodious tones and rhythms that mimicked the sounds of the ocean. Each word was a glimpse into their world, revealing secrets that echoed the undulating waves and the whispers of the deep. Leo listened intently, his heart swelling with a sense of belonging he had never felt before.

Furthermore, the merpeople introduced him to their customs, and rituals that celebrated the changing tides and the cycles of marine life. He learned about the majestic coral festivals, where vibrant colours danced in harmony with the currents, and the solemn ceremonies that honoured the spirits of the ocean. Every lesson enriched Leo's understanding, drawing him closer to the heart of this aquatic culture.

But perhaps most importantly, they imparted to him their vast knowledge of the ocean's secrets—its hidden treasures, its dangers, and its immeasurable beauty. Leo discovered how to read the signs of the sea, from the behaviour of the tides to the movements of the fish that swam in schools. He learned which waters were teeming with life and which shoals held hidden perils. With each revelation, Leo felt more connected to the ocean, as if he had become a part of it, woven into the very fabric of its existence.

As the bond between Leo and the merpeople deepened, so did his sense of purpose. He understood that he was not just a visitor in their world; he was becoming an integral part of it. Together, they would face challenges, protect the ocean they loved, and perhaps find a way to bridge the gap between their two worlds—one filled with air and the other with water. The adventure that awaited him was one woven with the threads of destiny, and he was ready to embrace all that it held.

With the guidance of the merpeople, Leo embarked on an extraordinary journey of self-discovery. Initially, he had merely thought of his unique ability to manipulate water as a fun skill—a way to play and create mesmerizing displays with the ocean's waves. However, the wise, ethereal beings of the sea opened his eyes to a deeper truth. Leo realized that his extraordinary talent carried significant weight; it was not just a frivolous pursuit, but a powerful tool imbued with the potential to protect the vast and fragile waters of the ocean and all its diverse inhabitants.

Inspired by the merpeople's profound reverence for their aquatic home, he began to see the ocean not just as a playground, but as a living entity that needed nurturing and care. Each wave he could summon, each tidal movement he could command, suddenly became a means through which he could bring about positive change. With this realization blossoming within him, Leo dedicated himself to using his gift for noble causes.

Leo's newfound purpose led him to collaborate closely with the merpeople, learning their ancient ways and the intricate balance of life beneath the surface. He soon found himself diving into the depths of the ocean with them, understanding the delicate ecosystems that thrived in coral reefs and the vital role that every creature played within these underwater realms. As he shared in their wisdom, he recognized the urgency of the challenges faced by the ocean—pollution, habitat destruction, and the plight of countless marine species in distress.

With renewed determination, Leo began to channel his abilities. He would gracefully swim alongside the merpeople, using his gift to aid healing efforts for injured sea turtles, entangled dolphins, and delicate fish populations suffering from the impacts of human intervention. With gentle waves of his hand, he could summon currents that guided lost creatures back to safety, energizing them with revitalizing water flows that promoted recovery and strength.

Moreover, Leo took it upon himself to advocate for conservation, inspiring others on land to protect the ocean as fiercely as its denizens did. He worked alongside the merpeople to plant coral fragments, regenerate habitats that had been ravaged by climate change, and educate those who ventured to the sea's edge about the importance of respecting and preserving the ocean's resources.

Through his efforts, Leo not only fostered a sense of unity between the human and merfolk worlds, but he also restored balance to the ocean's ecosystems. As he witnessed the once struggling habitats rejuvenate and thrive, he felt an overwhelming sense of fulfilment. The ocean was no longer just a beautiful playground; it had become a sanctuary worth fighting for, and he was honoured to play a part in its protection. His journey had transformed him, and Leo had truly become a guardian of the deep.

As Leo's reputation as a steadfast protector of the sea grew, so too did his deepening bond with the merpeople, the enigmatic denizens of the underwater realm. Their shimmering scales and graceful movements were a stark contrast to the chaos above, and they quickly came to see Leo not merely as an outsider, but as one of their own. To them, he was a guardian of the ocean, a champion who would fight valiantly to defend its breathtaking beauty and safeguard the myriad secrets hidden within its depths.

Leo's determination to protect the aquatic ecosystem endeared him to the merfolk, who began to share their ancient knowledge and traditions with him. They told stories of the ocean's vast expanse, of coral reefs that danced with colours more vibrant than any sunrise, and of creatures that could only be dreamed of by those who walked on land. The more he learned from them, the more he felt a sense of belonging, forging an unbreakable bond that transcended the barriers of land and sea.

However, not everyone shared this reverence for the ocean's wonders. Beneath the surface, there lurked a growing threat from those who were driven solely by greed and ambition. These exploiters, often equipped with modern technology and insatiable appetites for profit, sought to siphon off the ocean's resources for their gain, viewing it as a treasure trove to be plundered rather than a delicate ecosystem to be cherished. To them, Leo was nothing short of an obstacle—a formidable threat to their plans of exploitation and devastation.

While they revelled in the idea of harnessing the ocean's riches, Leo stood resolutely in their way, vowing to defend the very essence of the sea and all who inhabited it. This clash of ideologies set the stage for a battle not just for resources but for the soul of the ocean itself. Leo knew that he had the support of the merpeople behind him, their collective strength giving him hope and purpose. Together, they fought not only to preserve their home but to remind humanity of the profound interconnectedness of all living things and the importance of protecting the natural world. Thus, Leo's journey became a beacon of hope and resistance against the tide of greed that threatened to engulf the ocean he loved so dearly.

In the depths of the azure ocean, a notorious group of ruthless pirates, known for their insatiable greed and cunning tactics, had stumbled upon an ancient and long-forgotten underwater city, rumoured to be filled with treasures beyond imagination. Tales of glimmering gold, dazzling jewels, and artefacts imbued with magical properties had captured their attention, fueling their desire to plunder the city's riches. However, the pirates were not fools; they understood that the city was protected by powerful enchantments and formidable defences that had withstood the test of time.

Central to the protection of this magnificent underwater realm was a young hero named Leo. With a deep connection to the city and its magical essences, he possessed the unique ability to unlock its defences and manipulate the spells that kept out intruders. As the pirates meticulously devised their treacherous plan, they set their sights on capturing Leo, fully aware that without him, their chances of breaching the city and seizing its wealth were slim to none.

Unbeknownst to the pirates, Leo had allies among the merpeople, the guardians of the ocean depths who had watched over the city for centuries. When the merpeople learned of the pirates' nefarious intentions, they quickly sought out Leo, warning him of the imminent threat. In a secret gathering held in a hidden grotto illuminated by bioluminescent corals, the merpeople shared every detail of the pirates' plans, outlining the peril that awaited the city should the invaders succeed in capturing Leo.

Empowered by the knowledge of the impending danger, Leo felt a surge of responsibility and determination rise within him. He recognized that the very essence of the underwater city depended upon its defences and its connection to the sea. With the combined wisdom of the merpeople and his instincts, Leo began to formulate a strategy to protect both himself and the city. They devised traps and magical barriers, using the natural resources of the ocean to fortify their defences against the imminent onslaught.

As the sun dipped below the horizon, casting a golden hue across the waves, Leo gathered his thoughts and steeled himself for the confrontation ahead. With the support of the merpeople and an unwavering belief in his abilities, he prepared to stand against the ruthless pirates. Together, they would protect the underwater city and ensure that its treasures remained safeguarded from those who sought only to exploit and destroy. The battle for the future of their home was about to begin, and Leo was ready to face whatever challenges lay ahead.

The battle raged on with an intensity that electrified the air, a cacophony of clashing steel, cries of defiance, and the roaring of waves. The sound of cannon fire echoed across the tumultuous sea as the pirates launched their merciless assault, attacking from both the shadows of the depths and the daring heights above. Leo, at the centre of this storm, was a beacon of courage amidst the chaos. With his heart pounding in his chest, he stood resolute, channelling his extraordinary ability to manipulate water in a way that would turn the tide of battle in their favour.

As the pirate ships drew closer, their sails billowing ominously against the darkening sky, Leo focused intently. He could feel the pulse of the ocean beneath him, a living entity that responded to his will. With a powerful wave of his hand, he summoned a massive tidal wave, towering like a wall of liquid fury. It crashed down upon the approaching ships, enveloping them in a torrent that sent splintered wood and terrified pirates flying into the air. For a brief moment, the sea itself seemed to belong to him, a weapon forged of nature's essence.

But he would not stop there. Recognizing that chaos was his ally, Leo called upon the myriad of creatures that thrived beneath the surface, summoning shimmering schools of fish that darted about like silver arrows. With a flicker of his fingers, the fish surrounded the pirates like a swirling cloud, disorienting them with their sudden, frantic movements. The pirates, momentarily distracted by the unexpected assault from the depths, stumbled and faltered, losing precious moments in a battle where every second mattered.

The clash continued, filled with the roar of the ocean and the relentless struggle of men fighting for their lives. Yet, even amidst the chaos and the smell of salt and smoke, Leo stood firm, a determined guardian of the sea. With each wave he commanded, each creature he summoned, he felt a growing sense of purpose. This was not merely a fight against pirates; it was a fight for justice, for the freedom of the seas, and for all creatures who called it home. With each wave he conjured and every fish he sent forth, Leo knew he was not just protecting his allies but shaping the very course of the battle itself.

In the end, Leo and the courageous merpeople emerged victorious, successfully driving the ruthless pirates away from their underwater home. The epic battle had been intense, with fierce waves crashing and magic swirling through the deep blue sea. As the last of the pirate ships retreated into the distance, the inhabitants of the city rejoiced. Their homes were safe once more, and they celebrated with vibrant colours, music, and laughter echoing through the underwater caverns. Leo's bravery shone brightly throughout the conflict, and as the cheers of gratitude enveloped him, his reputation as a hero was solidified in the hearts of the merpeople and sea creatures alike.

Yet, even amid the celebrations, Leo couldn't shake the feeling that his journey was far from over. He gazed out at the horizon, the sun setting beautifully over the vast, mysterious ocean. He knew deep down that more challenges lurked beneath the surface, waiting for the right moment to emerge. The ocean was a living, breathing entity, filled with wonders and dangers alike. From ancient sea monsters that threatened the tranquillity of the coral reefs to environmental changes that could affect the delicate balance of marine life, Leo understood that his newfound role as a protector came with great responsibility.

With determination etched on his face, Leo resolved to continue his journey of safeguarding the ocean and its many inhabitants. Drawing strength from his victories and the friendships he had forged with the merpeople, he prepared himself for the trials that lay ahead. He would need to harness not only his courage but also his intelligence and resourcefulness. The ocean was vast, and its secrets were deep; Leo knew that to truly fulfil his destiny, he must be willing to explore uncharted territories, learn from ancient wisdom, and listen to the whispers of the waves.

As the moon rose high in the sky, casting silver light upon the water, Leo's heart pulsed with anticipation. He had become part of a greater narrative, one that united both the surface and the depths. With every fish that swam, every current that flowed, and every wave that crashed, he could feel the call to adventure beckoning him onward. Leo understood that he was not just fighting for a cause; he was fighting for the very essence of the ocean itself, and he was ready to embrace whatever challenges awaited him in the depths of the unknown.

Chapter 3

Leo's discovery of the shipwreck had ignited an insatiable fire of curiosity within the village, bringing a surge of enthusiasm for its long-forgotten maritime history. The older villagers, whose faces were lined with the stories of their ancestors, began to gather in the evenings, their hearths glowing with flickering flames and spirits lifted by camaraderie. They shared not just tales, but legends, rich and deep with intrigue—stories of the ship's origins were intertwined with the lore of a notorious pirate captain known as Captain Blood, who had once ruled these treacherous waters centuries prior. Whispers floated on the evening breeze, tales of a dark curse that had been cast upon the vessel, sealing the fates of its crew to the depths of the ocean, eternally bound to the wreckage that had become their tomb.

One crisp evening, as an orange glow filled the sky and the sun dipped below the horizon, Leo found himself seated by the fire, enthralled by the myriad stories wafting through the air. The words of the villagers twisted and danced like the flames themselves, carrying him away into a world of adventure and peril. Yet, amid the laughter and flames that cocooned him in warmth, Leo felt an unexpected sensation slither down his spine—an icy chill that whispered secrets of the past. He shivered, not from the cold, but from a vivid vision that struck him with unexpected intensity: there stood a striking woman, shimmering with an ethereal presence, her emerald eyes aglow and hair like raven silk cascading over her shoulders. She stood on the deck of the shipwreck, her expression a tempest of sorrow and ire, as if trapped in an eternal struggle, her gaze seemingly reaching right through the veil of time to pierce Leo's very soul.

Fear gripped Leo suddenly. This was no mere figment of his imagination, but a haunting encounter—a ghostly apparition of a sea witch, perhaps, bound by her own grief and fury to this forgotten vessel. The weight of her presence lingered, undeniably powerful and unsettling. Leo felt an overwhelming urge to delve deeper into the mystery that had unfolded before him, to understand the plight of these lost souls and to uncover the truth behind their tragic demise.

Motivated by a relentless curiosity and a burgeoning sense of empathy for the tormented spirits, Leo made a bold decision—to confront the sea witch herself. Under the shroud of night, with the moon stirring a silver path across the water, Leo returned to the shipwreck, his heart pounding with both trepidation and anticipation. As he drew closer, a sudden chill brushed against him, a cold wind sweeping across the water's surface, accompanied by an eerie, mournful wail that cut through the darkness like a siren's call.

There she was, the sea witch, manifesting from the shadows, her figure shimmering like a mirage in the moonlight. She appeared even more exquisite than he had imagined; her beauty cloaked in a haunting allure. But it was her eyes that captivated him—their luminosity unnerved him, filled with a tempestuous energy that hinted at an age-old sorrow.

"Why do you disturb the peace of the dead?" she demanded, her voice echoing like the howling wind, a stark contrast to the calm night around him.

With a steadying breath, Leo summoned the courage to express the truth of his intentions. "I wish to learn more about the shipwreck and its crew," he confessed, his voice unwavering despite the fear that danced within him. The sea witch regarded him while her fierce countenance softened, perhaps intrigued by the genuine compassion emanating from this young man, igniting a flicker of hope in the enduring darkness.

"The ship you see is the Black Diamond," she revealed, her tone imbued with nostalgia. "It was once a vessel of extraordinary power and prosperity, commanded by the ruthless Captain Blood, a man so consumed by greed and arrogance that it blinded him to the inevitable consequences of his actions. In the end, he and his crew were cursed by the very gods whose waters they pillaged."

Leo listened intently, enamored and horrified in equal measure. The tale unfolded, and with each word, he felt a deeper connection to the souls of the ship's doomed crew.

"The curse has trapped them within the shipwreck," she continued, her voice heavy with melancholy. "They are forever condemned to wander the ocean depths, cursed to never find solace, deprived of the peace they desperately seek."

A profound wave of sympathy washed over Leo, empathy for the lost souls tormented by their own misdeeds. He couldn't simply stand by and allow their fate to remain sealed in the depths of despair.

"Is there anything I can do to break the curse?" he implored, sincerity lacing his words as he reached out to the sea witch, desperate to uncover a path to redemption for the souls ensnared by this tragic fate.

The sea witch paused, her eyes shimmering with a strange illuminating light as she considered his proposition. The silence stretched, heavy with possibility and unspoken truths, as the waves lapped gently against the battered sides of the wreckage, echoing the unending call of the ocean.

"There is only one way," she replied, her voice echoing with an otherworldly resonance that sent shivers down Leo's spine. Her eyes, glimmering like the moonlight dancing on the waves, held a depth that spoke of untold mysteries. "You must embark on a quest to find the heart of the sea, a hidden treasure that lies beneath the turbulent waters, a treasure so powerful that it can break the chains that bind the souls of the Black Pearl's crew. But be warned, this treasure is fiercely guarded by the most fearsome creatures of the deep, beasts that have terrorized sailors for centuries."

Leo's heart raced at the thought of the perilous journey that lay ahead. He had heard the tales whispered in taverns, stories of monstrous leviathans with slimy tentacles that dragged ships down into the abyss, and schools of predatory fish with razor-sharp teeth that feasted on the unwary. Nevertheless, he felt a burning resolve inside him; the souls of those cursed sailors deserved salvation, and he was willing to risk everything to help them find peace.

He took a deep breath, steeling himself for the trials he would face. "Thank you," he said to the sea witch, his voice firm despite the uncertainty looming before him. "I will find the heart of the sea and end their suffering." Her gaze lingered on him for a moment longer, as if she was assessing the depth of his resolve.

With his heart pounding in his chest, he turned away from the flickering light of her cave and stepped into the salt-laden breeze of the open sea. The waves crashed against the shore, whispering secrets of the depths, urging him forward. He knew the task would be fraught with danger, but the thought of freeing the long-imprisoned souls fueled his determination. There was no turning back now.

As he walked away from the sea witch, her voice echoed hauntingly in his ears, imbued with a touch of optimism that lingered amidst the shadows of uncertainty.

"May the sea be with you, brave boy," she intoned, her tone both soothing and mystifying. "And may you find what you seek."

Leo paused for a brief moment, the glimmer of her blessing igniting a flicker of hope within him. He understood that the journey ahead would be fraught with peril—an adventure where danger lurked in every corner, waiting to ensnare the unwary. Yet, despite the myriad of challenges that lay ahead, he felt undeterred, compelled by an unquenchable desire to fulfill his mission. With the witch's words tugging at his spirit, he made his way back to the village, each step resonating with a newfound determination, as if the very ground beneath him vibrated with the promise of the quest ahead.

In the days that unfolded after his encounter with the sea witch, Leo immersed himself in the lore of his ancestors. He spent countless hours poring over ancient maps decorated with cryptic symbols and faded lines that spoke of uncharted waters and lost realms. His heart raced as he combed through ragged books filled with legends and tales—each story thrumming with the whisper of adventure that beckoned him nearer to the heart of the sea. The village elders, wise and weathered, became his mentors; they gathered around their fires at night, sharing riveting stories of mythical creatures that danced beneath the waves and treasures that sparkled like stars in the night sky. Their tales painted vivid images in Leo's mind, igniting his imagination and feeding his urgency.

After weeks of relentless searching, dedication bore fruit. The sun was setting low on the horizon when Leo encountered a sailor whose face was etched with the lines of countless voyages. The man's eyes twinkled with the glimmer of knowledge as he relayed whispers of a hidden underwater grotto, a place of mystery and peril where the heart of the sea was said to reside. He hesitated before mentioning the guardian of this sacred treasure—a fearsome sea serpent, a creature of legend that had prowled the ocean's depths for ages uncounted. The sailor's words sent a shiver down Leo's spine; he spoke of the serpent's immense power, hinting at its ancient wisdom and immeasurable wrath.

But Leo was resolute, undeterred by the sailor's warning. He felt a surge of brave conviction that gripped him like the tide pulling at the shore. He recognized that he could not accomplish this daunting quest alone. So, he sought out his most trusted companions: Silas, the rugged fisherman whose skills and bravery were known throughout the village, and Anya, a headstrong young woman whose bond with the ocean seemed almost mystical. Her affinity with the sea was profound, as if she could hear its secrets and understand its whispers, and she would be integral to their mission.

With their hearts set on their perilous journey, the trio gathered supplies and provisions, preparing to venture into the unknown. Under a sky that was a riot of colors, they set sail together, the wind catching their sails and thrusting them far out into the open sea, where they could leave behind the familiarity of land and step into the realm of adventure. As the days melded together, the horizon stretched endlessly before them, the ocean unfurling like a vast tapestry of blue, deep and mysterious.

Eventually, after a long voyage filled with laughter, worry, and the camaraderie that binds friends in times of uncertainty, they reached the fabled location of the hidden grotto. As they descended into the shimmering depths of the ocean, the water gradually became colder, a chilling embrace that tugged at their very beings. Shadows danced around them, and they marveled as strange, luminescent creatures flickered into view, their eyes glowing eerily in the enveloping darkness, casting an otherworldly glow that illuminated the path forward. Each flicker and shimmer in the abyss spoke of ancient secrets yet to be revealed, urging Leo and his companions deeper into the heart of the sea, closer to the adventure that awaited them.

Finally, after navigating through the winding underwater passageways and overcoming various obstacles, they reached the grotto. As they entered the cavernous space, a sense of awe washed over them. The walls were adorned with enchanting bioluminescent algae that glowed in various shades of blue and green, illuminating the grotto with an ethereal light. The soft, flickering illumination created a dreamlike atmosphere that danced across the damp surfaces, casting mesmerizing reflections in the still water.

In the heart of the grotto, coiled majestically around a massive pillar of coral, lay the sea serpent. The creature was nothing short of colossal, its immense body undulating gracefully as it shifted to observe the intruders. Its scales gleamed with a metallic sheen, catching the bioluminescent light and creating a captivating display of colors. The serpent's eyes, the size of dinner plates, were strikingly vivid, radiating a fierce and predatory light that pierced through the murky depths of the grotto. They seemed to hold an ancient wisdom and a threatening intelligence, scanning the room with keen interest.

Leo stood at the threshold of the grotto, knowing that he had to confront the formidable sea serpent. Yet, despite the creature's intimidating presence, he found himself devoid of fear. Instead, he was filled with a sense of determination and purpose. He recalled the words of the sea witch, her voice echoing in his mind like an incantation: "To free the lost souls of the Black Diamond crew, you must confront the guardian of these waters." Her warning had been clear, but so too had her promise—should he succeed, the souls trapped within the depths would be liberated, and their long-awaited freedom would be granted.

With the stakes set high and the weight of his mission pressing upon him, Leo took a deep breath and stepped further into the grotto. The sea serpent unfurled slowly, its massive form rising to its full height, and Leo knew that there was no turning back. The encounter he had dreaded yet anticipated was about to unfold, and he was ready to embrace whatever fate awaited him in this enchanted and perilous underwater realm.

With a deep breath, Leo steeled himself and stepped forward with determination. The towering figure of the sea serpent loomed before him, its iridescent scales shimmering ominously in the dim light. As it hissed, a low, guttural sound filled the air, echoing off the rocky cliffs surrounding them. The serpent reared its massive head, a fearsome sight that could intimidate any lesser soul. However, Leo stood resolute, his heart steady despite the danger that surrounded him. He focused intently on the pulsating heart of the sea, a small, radiant orb nestled securely within the serpent's sinuous coils. This orb, glowing with an ethereal light, seemed to hold the essence of life itself, calling to him in a way that was both enchanting and terrifying.

Drawing upon every ounce of strength and courage within him, Leo extended his hand toward the orb, desperation fueling his resolve. As his fingers brushed against its warm surface, the sea serpent reacted violently, lashing out in fury. Its muscular tail struck the water with thunderous power, sending torrents of waves crashing outward, creating ripples that spread across the surface like a wild dance. Despite the chaos, Leo's grip on the orb remained fierce and unyielding. He could feel the energy of the sea swirling around him, a tumultuous force that threatened to pull him under, but he was determined not to fail.

Time seemed to elongate as Leo clung tenaciously to the orb, his heart racing with each moment that passed. Finally, after what felt like an eternity, the sea serpent seemed to relent, easing its formidable grip. With a final surge of effort, Leo held the orb triumphantly in his hands, its light radiating warmth that permeated the cold ocean depths.

With the fabled heart of the sea now in his possession, clarity washed over Leo. He understood that he had broken the curse that had bound the souls of the Black Diamond crew to the depths of the ocean. A wave of relief and triumph surged through him. He turned towards his companions, a group of brave souls who had stood beside him through thick and thin, and signaled for them to follow him back to the surface. As they swam upward, their movements synchronized in a dance of hope, a sense of peace enveloped Leo. He knew they would soon emerge into the light of a new day, free from the shadows that had threatened to consume them.

When they finally breached the surface, the dawn was painting the sky with hues of orange and gold, the sun just beginning to rise over the horizon. The village, nestled against the shore, was awash in this golden light, transforming the familiar landscape into an ethereal scene. The air was rich with the sweet, invigorating scent of salt and seaweed, a promise of new beginnings and fresh opportunities. Leo and his companions swam toward the shore, their hearts swelling with joy and relief. They had not only saved the crew's souls but had also forged a bond of strength and resilience that would last a lifetime. As they stepped onto the warm sand, cheers erupted from the villagers who had gathered to witness the safe return of their heroes. In that moment,

Leo embraced his newfound identity as "The Boy Who Caught the Oceans," a title that carried with it the weight of adventure and the spirit of bravery.

The news of Leo's extraordinary victory spread like wildfire throughout the land, captivating the imaginations of all who heard it. From bustling towns to quiet villages, whispers of his bravery echoed in every corner of the realm. He was hailed as a hero, not just for his triumph over the formidable sea witch and her dark magic, but for the compassion he had shown to the souls who had long been trapped in despair. This young man, with a heart as vast as the ocean itself, had saved the lost and returned hope to those who had forsaken it.

With the sea witch's curse broken, a sense of tranquility enveloped the coastal regions. The once-turbulent waters of the Black Diamond shimmered with newfound clarity, and the dark clouds of fear and sorrow that had hung over the land for so long began to disperse. The ocean, now at peace, was a vibrant tapestry of life once more, teeming with colorful fish, dancing dolphins, and swaying kelp forests. Leo's name became synonymous with hope, his deeds inspiring songs and tales that echoed through taverns and marketplaces, immortalizing his legacy in the hearts of the people.

As the days turned into weeks, Leo continued to explore the enchanting depths of the ocean, his adventurous spirit unfazed by the challenges that lay ahead. Each dive revealed the breathtaking beauty of the underwater world—the brilliant coral reefs, the haunting shipwrecks, and the mesmerizing glow of bioluminescent creatures. Leo's love for the sea deepened with every exploration; he learned its secrets and forged a bond with its inhabitants. He became a legendary figure, not only for his bravery against the sea witch but also as a guardian of the ocean and a fierce protector of all marine life.

With time, Leo dedicated himself to safeguarding the waters he held so dear. He advocated for the preservation of marine ecosystems, educating others about the importance of respect and harmony between humans and the sea. Fishermen sought his counsel, children clamored for his stories of adventure, and even the most hardened sailors spoke of the boy who could catch the ocean in his hands. His spirit was indomitable, radiating courage and determination wherever he went.

And so, the tale of Leo lived on, a narrative woven into the very fabric of the community. He became a symbol of resilience, his actions a testament to the power of courage, determination, and the enduring spirit of the human heart. As the sun set over the calm ocean waves each evening, the people would often gaze out at the horizon, hoping to catch a glimpse of the young hero whose legacy would continue to inspire generations to come.

Chapter 4

The cool autumn breeze lovingly embraced the village of Seabrook Haven, making its way through the cobbled streets like a gentle guardian. It rustled the leaves of the ancient trees that stood as vigilant sentinels over the landscape, their gnarled branches reaching toward the sky as if in prayer. Each robust gust of wind sent cascades of leaves swirling gracefully through the air, transforming the scene into a breathtaking spectacle of nature. The leaves danced with abandon, presenting a dazzling display of vibrant gold, fiery red, and warm orange that seemed to shimmer against the backdrop of a crisp, azure sky. The sight was nothing short of magical, as though nature itself had decided to throw an extravagant celebration, inviting all who laid eyes upon it to fully immerse themselves in its beauty.

In this picturesque environment, laughter erupted from the children, their innocent joy filling the air with joyous shouts and cheerful shrieks. They darted around like energetic little whirlwinds, their small feet eagerly kicking through mounds of crispy, fallen leaves that carpeted the ground. Each determined kick sent a dynamic shower of foliage swirling into the air, creating whimsical clouds of brilliant colours that glittered in the soft sunlight like confetti from a parade. The children's carefree play was utterly infectious; their glee was a poignant reminder of life's simple joys. They built leaf piles high before launching themselves into the vibrant chaos, emerging time and again with triumphant grins that mirrored their unabashed joy.

As the scene unfolded, the villagers moved about with a palpable sense of contentment that seemed to blanket the town like a warm quilt. They scurried from one place to another, exchanging cheerful greetings and warm, friendly smiles as they attended to their daily tasks. The baker appeared from his cozy shop, the delicious aroma of freshly baked bread wafting behind him like an inviting embrace, while the alluring scent of pumpkin spice teased and tantalized from the local café, beckoning passersby to indulge. Neighbours took moments to pause and chat, sharing snippets of news and stories that wove a tapestry of connection, their voices blending into a harmonious symphony that celebrated the essence of community spirit.

Amidst this idyllic tapestry, Leo's laughter rang out like a chorus of joyful bells, brightening the already cheerful atmosphere even further. Each chuckle and giggle that escaped from him seemed to embody the very spirit of the season—he was a beacon of positivity in a world that often felt fraught with challenges and uncertainty. Recently, he had uncovered hidden talents within himself, each discovery sparking an overwhelming sense of excitement and boundless possibility. Whether it was painting vibrant landscapes, strumming melodies on a guitar, or spinning enchanting tales, each new endeavor he pursued added depth and richness to his existence, much like the vivid autumn leaves that filled the village.

This awakening not only elevated his spirits but also transformed his perspective on the world around him. The once-muted colours of his life became painted with vibrant strokes of creativity and unfiltered joy, igniting a sense of enthusiasm in those who surrounded him. His eyes sparkled with dreams yet to be realized, and every moment that passed felt ripe with potential, much like the golden leaves gently twirling in the refreshing autumn air. In Seabrook Haven, a place where laughter, community, and the wonders of nature intertwined, Leo began to understand that life's true magic lay in the profound ability to embrace the beauty woven into every single day.

However, the village was not universally welcoming of Leo's newfound exuberance. His ability to command the elements of joy sparked envy and jealousy among many of the townsfolk. The seeds of discontent began to sprout and fester, starting with whispered conversations—a dark cloud lurking ominously over the previously vibrant village, enveloped in sharp, thorny rumours. Those who felt overshadowed by Leo's radiant spirit slowly began to draw apart, their darkened hearts knitting together a web of resentment that threatened to tarnish the jubilant atmosphere of Seabrook Haven. As those whispers grew louder, the village stood on the precipice of a clash between joy and jealousy, testing the strength of its community bonds.

"Did you see how the rain ceased to fall when Leo danced around that tree?" a villager scoffed, arms crossed and eyes narrowed. "It's unnatural. He must've conjured it up!"

The words hung in the air like a heavy cloud, dampening the spirits of those nearby. This villager, a stout man with a weathered face and a deep scowl etched into his brow, looked around as if he were searching for allies among the gathered crowd. He leaned closer to another villager, hissing, "Sorcery! That's what it is, and sorcery brings misfortune! Do you remember old Mabel? She lost her chickens after he came prancing into the market."

Another villager, a woman with silver strands in her hair and a frown that hinted at decades of hardship, nodded emphatically. "Indeed! Ever since Leo arrived, strange things have been happening around here. Just last week, I found my prized tomatoes rotting on the vine. Did you see how the clouds turned dark and angry when he began to pluck those musical notes from his lyre?"

As the whispers of suspicion and jealousy swirled around them like the golden and crimson autumn leaves carried away by the brisk wind, Leo stood amidst the beauty of nature, focused and dedicated to honing his craft. Blissfully unaware of the simmering resentment that bubbled just beneath the surface of the community, he found solace beside the riverbank, where he would settle on the cool, grassy edge, his heart full of inspiration and creativity.

Day after day, and night after night, he immersed himself in his music, allowing it to flow freely as he strummed the strings of his cherished lyre. The gentle glow of twilight enveloped him, casting a warm golden hue over the landscape, which seemed to respond to his passion.

There, he would sing enchanting melodies, his voice flowing effortlessly into the evening air, weaving through the world like a gentle breeze that caressed every living thing in its path. Each note seemed to beckon the river itself to come alive, urging the water to dance gracefully in splashes of shimmering light that sparkled like diamonds under the fading sun.

The rhythms he created reverberated throughout the landscape, intertwining with the rustling of leaves and the whispers of the wind. The song had a way of binding the earth and sky together, a celebration of existence that echoed the harmony of all living things. With each deliberate pluck of the strings, it was as if he stirred the earth itself, igniting a quiet magic that drew forth flowers to bloom in vivid colours, even as the chill of autumn settled in and the days grew shorter and darker.

In this serene sanctuary, the air was thick with the scent of damp earth and the sweet fragrance of blooming wildflowers, painting an enchanting picture against the backdrop of the changing season. It was a wondrous sight, to witness vibrant petals unfurling against the backdrop of the impending winter, a testament to the beauty that could thrive even in challenging times. Each flower that blossomed was a shout of defiance against the cold, reminding all who passed that hope could still flourish amidst adversity.

Yet, as the villagers continued to gossip and cast wary glances towards him, Leo remained blissfully oblivious, lost in the magic of his own creation, unaware of the shadows creeping ever closer, threatening to cast a pall over his vibrant world. Little did he know, that the harmony he so passionately nurtured would soon clash with the discord sown by the murmurs of discontent and suspicion that rippled through the community like a winter chill.

Unbeknownst to Leo, as he poured his heart and soul into each of his performances, his extraordinary talent served to further ignite the simmering jealousy of those around him. They observed him from the shadows, their hearts heavy with an insidious mix of envy and longing, unable to grasp the pure, unadulterated joy and passionate exuberance with which he wholeheartedly embraced his art. For Leo, performing was never about seeking recognition or accumulating praise; it was simply a delightful celebration of life itself, a form of expression that allowed him to break free from the shackles of the mundane and routine that often weighed others down. However, in this enchanting simplicity, he inadvertently fanned the flames of rivalry among his peers, as they ached for a piece of the enchantment and magic he effortlessly wove into every note, every movement, and every word.

To Leo, his remarkable abilities transcended mere skills or technical mastery; they were a rare and precious gift bestowed upon him, a true testament to the profound and intimate bond he shared with the natural world that surrounded him. He possessed a unique and almost mystical connection to the elements, and with just a mere thought and a gentle gesture, he could summon the rain, providing nourishment to the parched crops that had long languished under the relentless embrace of a scorching sun. His hands, though seemingly ordinary, seemed to wield the power of the very skies themselves, drawing forth droplets of life-giving water that danced joyfully as they fell to the earth, nurturing the ground back to a state of vibrancy, fertility, and vitality.

In those moments, as the rain fell and the earth rejoiced, Leo felt a deep sense of fulfillment that was unmatched; it was a reminder of the importance of his craft, a calling that resonated within his very being. Yet, while he found solace in his unique talents, the shadows continued to grow darker around him. Those who witnessed his effortless connection to nature, who felt their own inadequacies rise to the surface in contrast to his brilliance, began to harbor resentment. They misunderstood the essence of his artistry, mistaking it for arrogance, and in their attempts to claim a piece of the wonder he embodied, they plotted and conspired, unable to appreciate the beauty of Leo's world.

Little did they know, Leo's journey was not one of self-importance, but rather an unfolding narrative of self-discovery, where each performance represented a step toward understanding his place within the grand tapestry of life. It was a journey that held the potential for collaboration and unity, where shared passions could lead to mutual respect and love for the art that connected them all. Still, as long as envy lingered like a dark cloud over his head, the risk of conflict and misunderstanding loomed large, casting a shadow over his luminous spirit.

In the darkest hours of winter, when the biting cold winds howled relentlessly and the world outside was blanketed in a harsh layer of frost, there existed an extraordinary figure named Leo. He possessed an almost mythical ability to summon warmth that spread across the land like a comforting embrace—a sanctuary of heat in an otherwise unforgiving season. With just a flick of his wrists and a gentle call to the elements, he would transform shivering fields, once devoid of life and color, into resplendent golden expanses that shimmered like freshly minted coins under the sun. He had the rare gift to turn harsh, frozen terrain into a welcoming haven, a tribute to the resilience and beauty of life itself.

The farmers, whose livelihoods and fates were intricately woven into the rhythms of nature's capricious dance, celebrated with exuberance the bountiful harvests that Leo helped bring about. Each year, their gatherings became vibrant festivals, echoing with the lively laughter that bounced through the fields and drifted on the breeze—a stark contrast to the dreary winter that surrounded them. Their smiles, bright and genuine, mirrored the joy and gratitude they felt for the abundance that had graced their lives through Leo's extraordinary influence. Yet, despite the outward expressions of happiness, a subtle shadow lurked just beneath the surface of their collective joy, insidious and unnerving.

For behind those jubilant faces, in the unguarded corners of their hearts, a seed of jealousy began to take root, dark and unnoticed, much like a weed thriving amid a flourishing garden. As they danced and sang praises of their good fortune, quietly, some farmers began to harbor thoughts that felt shameful and confusing. In the stillness of the night, during moments of quiet reflection, they found themselves wondering why Leo—a mere mortal—had been bestowed with such awe-inspiring power. How could one man wield the forces of nature in such an extraordinary manner, transforming their realities while they remained tethered to the labor of their own hands?

Their whispers filled the air like the breath of winter, soft and fleeting, but carrying heavy weight. They exchanged furtive glances amongst themselves, the unspoken questions hanging palpably in the breeze: Was Leo truly deserving of such gifts? Did he not, like them, have weaknesses, flaws, and fears? Although they donned masks of congratulations, shared in the abundant festivities, and raised their mugs in his honor, the insidious seed of envy continued to sprout, creating an unspoken divide among the villagers.

Deep within their hearts, the farmers wrestled with their own feelings of inadequacy and resentment that simmered just beneath the surface, threatening to spill over into their camaraderie. They felt a struggle within them—a tension between their gratitude for the blessings Leo brought and the gnawing sensation of being lesser in some intangible way. This conflict wove itself into their interactions, overshadowing their celebrations and painting their once-invincible bond with strokes of uncertainty and envy. In this web of emotion, the brilliance of Leo's gifts shone ever so brightly, casting long shadows into the depths of the farmers' hearts, where joy and jealousy began to dance an uneasy waltz.

As the seasons changed and the harvests thrived, painting the landscape in hues of gold and crimson, the townsfolk found themselves caught in a tumultuous internal struggle. While they outwardly applauded Leo's extraordinary talents and the bountiful rewards they brought to their community, lurking beneath their supportive façades was a simmering unrest—a quiet turmoil that gnawed at their hearts. They admired Leo's gifts, yes, but it was a double-edged sword; as they celebrated his successes, a part of them inevitably ached for a sense of connection they felt was forever just beyond their grasp.

This dichotomy of admiration and longing infused the air with an undercurrent of tension that subtly twisted the joyous atmosphere of their celebrations into something tinged with bitterness. Festivities that were meant to unite the townsfolk began to cast elongated shadows, and whispers of jealousy began to dance like mischievous phantoms amongst them. Those moments of joy became less about the occasion and more about Leo's apparent elevation above the rest—a reality that cast a pall over the very gifts he had shared so selflessly.

In a secluded corner of the village's tavern, Greta, the barmaid whose heart was as bitter as the stout she served, repulsively articulated the discontent swirling in the air. "That boy is too clever for his own good," she murmured, her voice laden with a sharpness that cut through the din of the tavern like a knife. Her words slipped from her lips with a venomous whisper, cloaked in jealousy, as she confided in herself, "He thinks he's above the rest of us, but I know the truth. He's playing a dangerous game!" The bite in her tone suggested a deeper resentment—an emotion nurtured not merely by envy, but cultivated through her keen observations of Leo's unsettling ascent to prominence within the community he had once belonged to.

Outside, in the bustling village square, Leo strode innocently among them, his gait imbued with the kind of self-assurance typically reserved for the gallant. Each confident step seemed to echo with the anticipation of the bright future that lay ahead, blissfully ignorant of the storm brewing in the hearts of those around him. His laughter, rich and melodious, rang out like sweet music, capturing the attention of passersby as sunlight cascaded around him, casting a warm glow that highlighted his youthful features, almost bestowing him with a celestial grace. Yet, as Leo moved through the streets, oblivious to the chaotic undercurrents of emotion swirling just beneath the surface, the smiles of the villagers morphed into tight-lipped expressions and reluctant grimaces. Their cheer, once genuine, soured into bitter masks, revealing the jealousy and skepticism that lay hidden behind their seemingly cheerful dispositions, casting an uneasy shadow over the bright moments they were meant to enjoy together.

Each sumptuous dish that simmered enticingly, emanating warmth and an array of spices from the bustling market, bore the unmistakable mark of Leo's extraordinary influence. This young man's exceptional talent for gastronomy had woven itself into the fabric of the local fare, elevating simple, everyday ingredients into breathtaking culinary masterpieces that dazzled the senses. Seasoned vendors proudly boasted of his unique recipes, speaking with utmost reverence about how his discerning palate had transformed their humble offerings into delights that patrons clamored for. Yet, amid the vibrant atmosphere filled with lively chatter and the rhythmic calls of shrewd bargaining echoing through the market stalls, a subtle yet palpable undercurrent of tension simmered just beneath the surface.

While many villagers gathered close to celebrate Leo's burgeoning prowess, clapping him on the back and calling out his name with unrestrained admiration, others lingered in the shadows at the fringes of the crowd. Their expressions were grave, brows furrowed in concern, eyes narrowed as they observed the unfolding scene with a cautious skepticism. The camaraderie shared between the supporters of Leo contrasted starkly with the apprehension largely palpable among the dissenters.

These wary villagers exchanged furtive glances, their silent communication a powerful language of shared unease. Each frown and furrowed brow was a poignant reminder of the unsettling reality that Leo's cleverness had disrupted the established norms they had come to rely upon. Whispers drifted through the air like a gentle but ominous breeze, insinuating that his remarkable talents, far from being a blessing, represented a potential threat to their way of life. They found themselves caught in a tangled web woven from envy and fear, speculating nervously about how far Leo's ambitions might lead him, and at what cost to their own stability and livelihoods.

And so, as Leo navigated his way through the vibrant throngs of the marketplace, the villagers' discomfort transformed into a growing tension. There lingered a weighty question: would his cleverness ultimately steer them all into an unforeseen downfall? Would he scale heights so extraordinary that they would feel forever trapped in the shadows, while their very livelihoods dangled precariously in the balance? Each unspoken thought twisted and turned in the air, filling the atmosphere with a suffocating heaviness, as they contended with the dichotomy of admiration for his talent and a creeping apprehension about his potential to upend their familiar world. The boy who danced jubilantly through the town square, exuding a spirit of carefree exuberance, in their eyes transformed into a harbinger of change—a change that threatened to overturn the delicate equilibrium of their existence.

As days morphed into weeks, the initial whispers echoing through Seabrook Haven gradually evolved into a tumultuous chorus of discontent, resonating restlessly along the quaint, cobbled streets. What had begun as tentative murmurs rife with uncertainty and fear burgeoned into a fervent storm of rumors that escalated disproportionately, intertwining to construct intricate narratives that painted Leo as something more sinister than he ever intended to be. The villagers, driven by a tumult of imagination and the daily anxieties that plagued their lives, began to weave fantastical tales of his alleged malevolence, depicting him not merely as an outsider but as a conjurer of dark magic—a sorcerer in their midst whose very presence seemed unjustly blamed for every misfortune that unfolded in their once-peaceful lives.

And thus, the transformation of Leo from a celebrated culinary innovator to a sinister figure in the eyes of the villagers played out like a tragic saga, unveiling the fragile boundaries between admiration and fear, creativity and devastation, bringing to light the complexities of human nature as they grappled with the ramifications of change in their midst.

In the troubled minds of the villagers, Leo had tragically transformed into the archetypal scapegoat, a figure onto whom they could project their collective frustrations and fears, an unfortunate victim of their own making. He stood as the embodiment of their shared anxieties—the perennial target who took the brunt of their misfortunes and misgivings. Each day that passed, the belief took deeper root among them, a vine of irrationality spiraling out of control, suggesting that he possessed powers far beyond their understanding or comfort. With time, their superstitions entwined with this newfound belief, crafting a sinister narrative around him that painted him as a harbinger of disaster.

Storms that swept through their humble village were no longer merely acts of nature but were construed as manifestations of his supposed wrath. Unfortunate accidents that plagued the community were attributed to his malevolence, seen as intentional acts meant to sow chaos amongst the lives of the innocent. Even the specter of failed crops, a serious blow to their livelihood, became an item of judgement against him, interpreted as a divine punishment orchestrated by Leo's dark hand. In their desperate need for a scapegoat and an explanation for the trials that beset them, the villagers grasped tightly to this dangerously simplistic narrative, wrapped in fear and misunderstanding—convinced in their hearts that Leo harbored sinister intentions.

Then came a fateful night, charged with an almost electric atmosphere of tension and uncertainty that seemed to seep into the very soil of Seabrook Haven. As night fell, it brought with it a thick blanket of unease, as if the stars themselves were trying to hide from the nuisances unfolding below. Overwhelmed by the waves of ignorance and suspicion that had engulfed the village, the residents, driven by fear and a desire for retribution, gathered in a tight circle at the town square, the very heart of Seabrook Haven. The air around them felt heavy, thick with emotions that ran the gamut from rage to fear, casting a cloud over the gathering that appeared to weigh down on their shoulders.

With each hesitant step Leo took toward the throng, his heart raced, pounding against his chest like a frantic drum, each beat echoing his apprehension. He could feel the intensity of their gazes upon him, the weight of their judgment palpable and oppressive, piercing through the cool night air like daggers of disdain aimed straight at his heart. Whispers danced on the wind, questions formed like shadows in the depths of their minds, each one adding to the mounting pressure that surrounded him. Leo's pulse quickened, not just from fear but from the realization that he was standing on the brink of something far greater than himself—a reckoning raised from the embers of suspicion and ignited by the need to find a culprit for their unrelenting hardships.

As the crowd murmured and fumed, Leo punctured the heavy veil of silence that clung to the atmosphere, feeling both the weight of their expectations and the desperation in their pleas for answers. He was determined to confront the storm that had brewed around his name, but the gathering loomed larger than just the physical presence of the townsfolk; it was a culmination of their shared tragedies, their cumulative grief woven into a fabric of blame that now tightly encased him. Leo stood on that precipice, caught between the shadow of accusation and the flickering light of truth, contemplating the fate that lay ahead.

As he approached the gathering, a sense of foreboding washed over him, intensifying with each hesitant step. The scene that unfolded before him was unsettling, sending an icy shiver rippling down his spine. A congregation of shadowy figures loomed in the dim light, their forms barely discernible, shrouded in an ephemeral cloak of darkness that seemed to pulsate with their unease. The flickering glow of the torches cast distorted shadows on the ground, making the situation feel even more surreal, as if he had wandered into a nightmare from which there was no escape.

Though their faces remained largely obscured, he could perceive the outlines of their expressions—etched deeply with a blend of contempt and hostility. The air was thick with tension, a density that seemed to seep into his very bones. He could almost hear the synchronized pulse of the crowd, a cadence tinged with both fear and anger, resonating like a drumbeat in the stillness of the night. They formed an impenetrable line, a resolute wall of suspicion that stood firm against him. Their penetrating gazes ignited a fierce inferno of resentment within him, igniting old wounds and fears from long ago, as their collective disdain threatened to engulf him entirely.

Caught in this whirlwind of emotion, Leo wrestled with an array of feelings that swirled chaotically inside him. Fear gripped him with cold fingers, a fear of what he once considered his home, a place that now felt alien and unwelcoming. Fury bubbled beneath the surface, a primal response to the betrayal he felt from those who should have been kindred spirits. But underlying all of these emotions was a profound sadness, a deep and abiding sorrow for the community he had once cherished—the very community that now loomed before him, fueled by a toxic blend of ignorance and prejudice.

Suddenly, amid the oppressive atmosphere, a voice broke through the silence, growling like distant thunder. "It's true, isn't it, Leo?" It was Ewan, the blacksmith, whose presence carried a weight that was felt even beyond his towering figure. His voice rumbled through the crowd, tinged with a mixture of weariness and palpable disdain. Ewan's hands, worn and calloused from countless years of tireless labor, bore testament to the harsh realities of life. He was a man forged and tempered in the crucible of hardship, yet it was the burden of his heart that seemed the heaviest—loaded with the burdens of suspicion and an ever-thickening sense of betrayal.

"You think you can bring change, but you are the curse that has fallen upon us!" Ewan's voice rose, sharp and vehement, echoing like a battle cry among the terrified villagers. His words struck Leo like arrows, each one a cruel reminder of the fears that had taken root and flourished in the hearts of those he once considered friends. "You're the reason crops have withered and the skies have darkened!" The accusation hung in the air, a stark indictment that reverberated through Leo's mind, further entrenching the divide that had so swiftly and irrevocably formed between him and the only community he had ever known.

As the words settled in the space between them, the severity of the moment crashed upon Leo like a violent wave, sweeping him into the depths of despair. Here he stood, a man no longer welcomed, confronting a community transformed—not by his actions, but by their own unfounded fears and obsessions with blaming others for their plight. The flickering torchlight cast a harsh glow on the gathering, and as the shadows writhed around him, it became painfully evident that a chasm had opened between him and the life he once cherished.

Gasps rippled through the crowd, a wave of surprise and collective indignation that swept over the gathering like a sudden gust of wind, unsettling the air and chilling the atmosphere. The sharp intake of breath echoed in the silence that followed, each gasp a testament to the disbelief that surged through the hearts of those assembled. Eyes widened in shock, brows knitted tightly in confusion and contempt; the accusation had struck home, penetrating deep into the minds of the villagers who had once considered Leo a friend and ally.

Leo stood at the center of this tempest, feeling the world around him tilt and spin as the harsh reality of the moment sank in. His throat tightened painfully, constricting his ability to speak, as if the very air had become thick and heavy. The words he longed to convey, to defend himself, clung stubbornly to the back of his mouth like stones lodged in the depths of his stomach, choking him. Each moment stretched out like an eternity, as he grappled with the overwhelming feelings of betrayal and despair washing over him.

He knew, deep down, that he couldn't hope to win against the tempest of anger and accusation that surged through the hearts of the villagers. Their expressions, once full of warmth and camaraderie, had morphed into harsh masks of suspicion and rage. With each harsh breath he took, he felt the weight of their gaze bearing down on him like a relentless storm, every pair of eyes a piercing reminder of the chasm that had opened between him and those he had once thought of as family.

The enormity of the moment pressed upon him, amplifying the sense of isolation that threatened to engulf him. Memories of laughter shared and trust forged flashed before his mind's eye, now tainted by the bitter poison of this singular accusation. Leo's heart raced as he realized that whatever bonds had held them together seemed to fracture and splinter before him, leaving him vulnerable and exposed amidst the tide of outrage.

As shouts began to echo and the crowd's fervor swelled, he could feel the very foundation of his existence shaking. Would he be able to navigate this treacherous sea of emotions? Could he salvage some semblance of the friendship he had cherished, or would the weight of misunderstanding and betrayal drown him in their midst? The questions clawed at him as the gale of indignation whipped through the gathering, leaving him teetering on the brink of despair, desperately searching for a lifeline in the tempest.

"I've only tried to help, Ewan," he finally managed to plead, his voice quivering yet rising with determination above the clamour of the crowd. With each word, he felt the weight of their gazes pressing down on him, the skepticism palpable in the air like a thick fog that refused to lift. "All I want is to share the gifts that nature has bestowed upon me. I am no sorcerer; I am but a friend to the earth!" He paused, inhaling deeply as he drew strength from the very soil beneath his feet, the essence of life that pulsed through the world around him. Leo's heart raced, a wild drumbeat echoing in his chest, as he desperately searched the faces surrounding him—each one a canvas painted with their own fears, hopes, and anxieties.

He scanned the crowd, hoping to find even a glimmer of understanding amid the tempest of disbelief swirling like leaves in a storm. There, amidst the sea of uncertainty, he spotted a familiar face—an old neighbor who once shared stories with him under the shade of the ancient oak tree. Yet even in her gaze, he could see the shadows of doubt and fear etched into every line of her skin, a reflection of the harsh realities they had faced in recent months. The drought had crept in like an unwelcome intruder, and the storms had ravaged their crops, leaving devastation in their wake. Still, Leo refused to be silenced, his spirit refusing to bow to the tide of despair that threatened to engulf them all.

"We've lived in harmony with the land for generations," he continued, his voice stronger now, fueled by the conviction that this knowledge was a beacon of hope in the darkness. "And I only wish to enhance that bond—to show you the paths of healing that nature can offer. The drought, the storms, they are not my doing," he implored, gesturing passionately towards the horizon, where the sun fought valiantly to break through the dark clouds that loomed ominously above. "These are natural cycles, yes, but with understanding and care, we can nurture our homeland back to its former glory."

His words echoed in the silence that followed, a soft entreaty against the rising tide of anxiety. Each syllable was carefully woven with threads of possibility, of connection, and of shared responsibility. "We stand at a crossroads," he added, his voice infused with urgency. "We can choose to wallow in our fears or embrace the knowledge that has been handed down through the generations. Together, we can learn to read the signs the earth gives us, to listen to her whispers, and in turn, we can heal her wounds."

As he spoke, the wind shifted, and for a fleeting moment, it seemed as though the world held its breath, allowing his words to hang in the air like the perfume of blooming wildflowers. Leo pressed on, hoping to ignite a flicker of revelation among them. "What if I could show you how to work with the land, to coax the rain from the clouds and nurture the soil back to life? Imagine a future where our children reap the harvests of our cooperation with nature, where the cycles that once brought fear are transformed into seasons of abundance."

He took a step closer to the crowd, matching their stares with unwavering resolve. "Change begins with us, right here, right now. If you open your hearts and minds to these ancient teachings, we can discover the harmony that lies within the natural world, and with it, reclaim our prosperity."

His words hung in the air, heavy with a tangible mix of hope and desperation, reverberating through the hearts of those who gathered around him. The crowd, a tapestry of weary faces and conflicted emotions, listened intently. Yet skepticism lingered in the atmosphere like a dark cloud, their suspicions rooted deep, far more profound than any fleeting complaints carried on the winds of discontent. Ewan, a man of the soil whose hands bore the scars of toil, fixed his unwavering glare on Leo, his expression hardening like the iron he forged in the embers of his workshop.

"You may call it nature," Ewan spat, his voice filled with a fervor that commanded attention, "but we see it as misfortune—a misfortune that began the moment you set foot in our village." His voice rose, fervent and relentless. "You preach of harmony and balance, yet our fields cry out for rain, parched and withering under the relentless sun. The winds that sweep through our lands now carry whispers of despair, echoing the feelings that lie heavy in our hearts."

With that, murmurs erupted among the villagers like rolling thunder—a cascade of voices that rose and fell, creating a symphony of discord. Some nodded in vigorous agreement with Ewan, their brows furrowed with shared frustration, while others appeared torn, caught in the tumultuous crossfire of loyalty to an old friend and the pervasive fear of the unknown looming like a shadow over their lives.

Leo stood in the center of it all, a lone figure navigating the swelling tide of emotions that ebbed and flowed around him, each wave filled with grief, anger, and an aching sense of loss. His heart raced as he took in the sight of familiar faces twisted with pain and uncertainty. He could feel the weight of their despair pressing down on his shoulders, and he prayed fervently that somehow, amid the cacophony of doubt and disillusionment, he could steer their hearts back toward hope, before the light of their shared dreams flickered out completely, swallowed by the darkness of their fears.

He cleared his throat, ready to speak, his voice steady though it trembled with the enormity of the moment. "I know the land suffers," Leo began, his gaze sweeping over the crowd, searching for the glimmers of understanding in their eyes. "But we must not let despair define us. Together, we can find solutions—together, we can heal this rift. I am of this village; I am with you, not against you." A silence enveloped the crowd, heavy yet pregnant with possibilities, and Leo felt a flicker of hope igniting within his chest. Perhaps, just perhaps, he could bridge the chasm between them all.

But their ears were closed, their minds firmly made up, locked in place like ancient stones weathered by the relentless passage of time. The air was thick with the murmurings of suspicion, swelling menacingly like a rising tide, far more powerful than any reasoned argument Leo could muster in his defense. Despite his best efforts, no amount of carefully structured logic or heartfelt appeals could slice through the dense fog of fear that had settled heavily upon them. It was as if a veil had been cast over their perceptions, thick and impenetrable, obscuring any glimmers of understanding or compassion that might still have lingered in their hearts.

Encouraged by their selfish dread of the unknown, an insidious shadow crept over the crowd, warping their familiar features into masks of hostility and distrust. They turned on him with a ferocity reminiscent of a swarm of angry bees, their fear igniting into a wildfire of accusations and anger that crackled through the night air. Cries of retribution erupted amongst the throng, filling the atmosphere with an oppressive weight, a palpable tension that felt almost suffocating as it echoed into the chilly evening.

"You bring only bad luck!" shouted Greta, her voice commanding and sharp, slicing through the chaos like a well-aimed arrow. Her fists were raised defiantly, trembling with a fervor that was both alarming and fierce, like a warrior readying for battle. Her stance radiated righteous indignation, as though she believed she was the herald of justice in an unjust world. "We'll be rid of you before you unleash more of your chaos!" The intensity of her words struck Leo like daggers, aimed directly at his heart, intending not just to wound but to instill an overwhelming sense of fear and urgency, to chase him away into the void from whence he had come.

The crowd surged behind her, emboldened by her fervor, and their voices melded into a cacophony of outrage. The air crackled with tension, and Leo felt the weight of their collective scorn pressing down on him. Each word hurled in his direction felt like a boulder, relentless and crushing, and he stood alone, a solitary figure amidst a sea of enmity. He longed to reach out, to bridge the gap that fear had carved between them, but the chasm only widened with every accusing gaze cast his way. In that moment, the sense of betrayal and isolation washed over him like a cold wave, threatening to pull him under into the depths of despair.

With a heart brimming with sorrow and disbelief, Leo cast a lingering glance at the faces that had once been integral to his world—friends with whom he had shared moments of laughter, joy, and camaraderie. But now, those cherished memories were grotesquely reshaped by the dark specter of fear that loomed over their interactions. Each familiar visage, once a canvas of trust and affection, was now marred by growing mistrust and resentment, shadows of suspicion flickering in their eyes. The genuine friendships that had flourished in the light of shared experiences had twisted insidiously into something sinister, a painful reminder that fear is a powerful manipulator, capable of distorting perceptions and unraveling even the strongest of bonds.

He turned on his heel, feeling an unbearable weight pressing down upon him, the collective animosity in the air palpable and suffocating. Each step he took felt like a retreat from the comfort of companionship he had once known. As he fled into the cover of the darkened woods, Leo felt as if he were escaping not just from the eyes of those who had turned against him, but also from the memories that had now become a source of anguish. Tears slipped from his eyes, shimmering in the silvery light cast by the moon, each one glistening like a star that had fallen from the sky, yearning to find its place once again. With every step he took, he felt an additional weight settle on his heart, like shackles binding him to the ground, severing him from the fleeting sense of belonging that had once felt like a warm embrace, now cruelly replaced by a fierce bitterness.

As he reached the very edge of the forest, where the trees stood tall and unwavering, resembling ancient sentinels guarding sacred secrets, Leo paused to listen intently. He hoped to find solace amidst the stillness, a reprieve from the turmoil that brewed within him. Silence enveloped him, save for the gentle rustling of leaves stirred by an unseen breeze and the eerie, haunting cry of an owl in the distance—a solitary sound that mirrored his own desolation, echoing through the night and amplifying his sense of isolation. Yet, even amidst this overwhelming despondency, he felt a soft, warm presence wrap around him, a sensation that was both familiar and profoundly comforting.

"My child," whispered a voice that floated through the air as softly as the breeze itself, weaving through the branches with a tender grace that seeped into his bones. It was the spirit of the woods, an embodiment of nature's heart, resonating with the essence of life, renewal, and the utter resilience of existence. "You cannot allow their hatred to extinguish the light that resides within you," it continued, each word a soothing balm to his weary soul. "Remember, flowers can still bloom through the cracks in stone." The spirit's ethereal voice enveloped him, anchoring him in the moment and reminding him of the persistent beauty of resilience that can thrive even in the harshest of environments.

With renewed determination kindling within him, Leo stood tall, embracing the shadows cast by the towering trees and the heavy expectations placed upon him by the world. Though the villagers' jealousy had left him with a heart that felt as heavy as boulders, the gentle light of the spirit began to soothe his unease, igniting a spark of hope within the recesses of his spirit. "You are so much more than their whispers," the spirit urged, wrapping him in an embracing cloak of reassurance. "You are a beacon of hope and connection in a world that often forgets its own light. Nature has chosen you for a reason. Embrace who you are and stand proud."

In that moment, Leo understood: he was not defined by the fear and animosity that had seeped into the hearts of those he once cherished. Instead, he was a conduit of light amidst the darkness, a bridge between fear and acceptance, and amidst the shadows of uncertainty, he found the courage to own his identity and the strength to rise above the darkness.

At that pivotal moment, the fear that had threatened to engulf Leo began to dissipate, like mist retreating before the strength of the morning sun. The unsettling apprehension that had clung to him, making his heart race and his mind whirl, slowly transformed into a burgeoning sense of purpose that filled him with warmth and determination. Taking a deep, grounding breath, Leo consciously connected to the pulse of the earth beneath his feet—a steady, reassuring rhythm that reminded him he was part of something far greater than himself.

The dense woods surrounding him, once silent and foreboding, seemed to awaken with life. Each rustle of leaves, each whisper of the wind, became a gentle encouragement, urging him to reclaim his belief in himself. The vibrant hues of green and the earthy scents of the forest enveloped him, recharging his spirit and igniting a fire within. Feeling this renewed strength surge through his veins, he realized that his journey before him was not merely about his own path; it was a quest to inspire others to open their hearts and minds to the beauty and interconnectedness of existence.

With this conviction deepening within him, Leo firmly planted his feet on the ground, centering his thoughts and emotions in the midst of the chaos that had once held him captive. He understood clearly now that the weight of the countless rumors swirling around him, much like a tempestuous storm, would no longer dictate his actions or overshadow his resolve. He was determined to confront those misconceptions not with words steeped in anger or defensive remarks but with the quiet strength of his heart and the profound depth of his spirit.

In that realization, Leo found clarity; mere verbal explanations, laden with frustration and hurt, would do little to mend the rift that had developed between him and the villagers. What they truly yearned for was not a justification of his actions, but rather an experience—a demonstration of the deep, intrinsic beauty and delicate balance of nature itself. He understood that by sharing this wonder with them, he could bridge the gap that had formed, fostering understanding and connection in a way that transcended words, sparking empathy and appreciation in their hearts. Thus, Leo resolved to become a conduit for the natural world's magic, showcasing its splendor to those who might learn to stand beside him in harmony and acceptance.

In his mind's eye, Leo envisioned the vibrant colors of the forest at sunrise, where rich oranges and soft pinks spilled across the sky like paint on a canvas, illuminating every leaf and petal in a warm embrace. He imagined the delicate dance of leaves as they fluttered gracefully in the gentle breeze, their rustling whispers woven into the air like a soothing lullaby. Alongside this picturesque scene, the harmonious sound of a babbling brook could be heard, weaving its way through the lush landscape, the water sparkling as it caught the morning light—each droplet a tiny gem reflecting the beauty of the world around it. It was this same unparalleled beauty that coursed through his veins, an innate power he had been blessed to wield. He had come to understand that this gift was not one that should incite fear or pain among the villagers, but rather a tool—an opportunity to serve as a bridge to healing and a pathway toward mutual understanding and acceptance.

As the first light of dawn broke once again over Seabrook Haven, casting a warm golden glow upon the quaint village that lay nestled between pristine hills, the villagers stirred from their slumber, greeted by the promise of a new day. This was not just another day; it was a second chance for them to open their eyes to the truth that had always been present but had often remained obscured by doubt and misunderstanding. It was the pivotal moment for Leo to step forward and reclaim his rightful place among them, not as an outcast cloaked in the shroud of jealousy, but as a steadfast friend—a devoted guardian of the beautiful earth they all shared, and an advocate for the wonder that surrounded them.

With each resolute step he took toward the heart of the village, Leo could sense the tension in the air beginning to dissipate like mist in the morning sun. Each breath filled him with resolve as he prepared to invite the villagers on a journey—a chance to witness the wonders of nature that inspired him, to delve into the intricate tapestry of life that signified the interconnectedness of all living things. He sought to open their hearts and minds, to help them realize that his powers were not a source of division, but rather a profound gift meant to nurture, restore, and enhance the world they inhabited together.

This was his moment to step into the light, to shine brightly and embody the spirit of Seabrook Haven. In doing so, he would stand as a living testament to the inherent beauty that existed both in the world around them and in the potential of the bonds they could strengthen if only they chose to embrace each other with compassion and openness. Leo's heart raced with anticipation as he prepared to share his truth, determined to foster a sense of unity that would envelop the village, reminding them all that they were stronger when they stood together, shoulder to shoulder, side by side.

Chapter 5

The horizon was a breathtaking canvas of shifting hues, glowing brilliantly with the fading colors of the sunset, which softly illuminated the peaceful village of Seabrook Haven. As the sun dipped lower, rich oranges and deep purples melded together seamlessly, casting an ethereal glow over the quaint cottages that dotted the landscape like gems scattered across a richly-coloured tapestry. Each structure, with its thatched roofs and ornate window boxes overflowing with vibrant wildflowers, seemed to bask in the warmth of nature's final farewell to the day. The scent of salt lingered in the air—a constant, comforting reminder of the ocean's proximity—mingling with the cool crispness of the approaching night, contributing to an invigorating atmosphere that hinted at the day's tranquil end and the mysterious adventures that awaited on the morrow.

As the final rays of sunlight dipped below the horizon, painting the sky with a soft twilight, fishermen busied themselves along the docks, diligently stowing their nets. Their strong, calloused hands moved with a practiced grace, deftly folding the heavy fabric of their nets as they prepared to leave the seas behind for the night. Laughter echoed from nearby, where children with flushed cheeks chased one another along the shore, their joyous shouts piercing the calmness of the evening and intermingling delightfully with the soothing sounds of the gentle waves lapping against the shore. The evening tide, rhythmic and hypnotic, created a soothing symphony that enveloped the village in a serene embrace, each wave rolling in harmony with the soft whispers of the salty breeze.

Among this lively village scene stood a figure of significant presence—a man whose very essence seemed to be intertwined with the sea itself. Leo, the revered sea mage, was not merely a local figure of legend; he was the guardian of the ocean's mysteries and its unpredictable ferocity, a protector not only of mankind but also of the countless creatures that thrived beneath the waves. His long, flowing robes mirrored the mesmerizing colors of the ocean, shifting from deep blue to shimmering green as he moved with grace, each step a testament to his deep connection with the maritime world. His hair danced in the wind like seaweed swaying beneath the surface, reflecting the spirit of the waters he cherished so deeply.

As Leo savored the twilight and its striking beauty, a sudden commotion shattered the tranquil atmosphere, pulling him from his reverie. A group of sailors staggered into the village, their clothes tattered and drenched, faces drawn and weary, and their eyes wide with desperation—a silent plea that spoke volumes of their harrowing journey. This ragged ensemble of men, their bodies shaking with exhaustion and fear, looked disheveled yet remarkably determined. One of them, a burly man with tangled hair and a weathered hat that bore the marks of countless storms, stepped forward, his breath coming in ragged gasps as he fought against the overwhelming weight of his desperation.

"Help us, please!" he gasped, his voice hoarse and urgent, laden with the fight for survival. "We've come from the ship, Dawnstar! We were caught in a storm beyond belief! Our vessel is crippled, and we've lost many of our crew in the chaos. We're terrified we won't make it back home without assistance." His plea hung thickly in the air, heavy with the gravity of impending catastrophe, and Leo felt a sinking sensation in his heart in response. Time and again, he had witnessed the destructive fury of the ocean, a tempest capable of bringing even the most seasoned sailors to their knees, stripping them of hope and dreams in mere moments. The vast body of water was both majestic and merciless—a force of nature that demanded unwavering respect.

"What of the others?" Leo asked, his voice steady even as a current of urgency throbbed beneath, quickening his pulse and igniting an internal alarm urging him to act at once.

"We were flung overboard in the chaos," the sailor continued, visibly trembling as he replayed the harrowing events in his mind, the horror of it etched in the lines of his face. "Some of our crew were lost to the depths; others swam to shore like we did. But our ship... it's beyond repair without powerful magic." He gestured toward the horizon, where dark memories loomed—the shadows of what had once been. Leo's heart raced at the thought; he knew the Dawnstar had been a magnificent ship, gliding through the waters with grace and elegance, leaving behind tales of bravery and adventure. Now, its fate and that of its crew teetered perilously on the edge of hope and despair, waiting for someone to reach out and restore what the tempest had taken away. Leo understood that he had to act, the weight of the ocean's call pressing upon him like the deep seas themselves, urging him to dive into action before it was too late.

"I will help," Leo declared, his voice ringing with an unwavering resolve that echoed over the gentle lapping of the waves. A surge of determination welled up inside him, powerful and fierce, reminiscent of the swell of the seas preparing for a tempest. It was as if the very essence of the ocean coursed through him, igniting a fire within his heart. "But you must be prepared for a challenge," he continued, his tone heavy with the weight of truth. "The sea does not give its treasures easily, nor does it yield to the faint of heart."

His words hung in the salt-laden air, laden with gravity and significance, emphasizing the profound respect one must nurture for the vast, unpredictable ocean. It was a living force, ancient and wise, demanding not just courage but relentless willpower when faced with its daunting depths. The sailors felt the seriousness of his message resonate within them, a reminder that they were not merely embarking on a quest for fortune; they were entering a realm where nature would test their strength and commitment.

A barb of uncertainty pricked the spirits of the sailors, a flicker of doubt that initially threatened to dim their collective resolve. Yet, in that moment of vulnerability, resolute nods passed among them like an unspoken understanding, a bond forged through shared dreams and past struggles. They understood the stakes, for they had come too far to even consider turning back. With a firm nod, Leo beckoned them forward, his eyes glinting with purpose as he led them toward the shoreline, that sacred place where the land kissed the water, and where destiny, like a tapestry of fate, awaited their eager embrace.

As they approached the water's edge, the air thick with anticipation and electric energy, Leo raised his arms, feeling the pulse of the universe respond to his command. The summer breeze began to whip around them, swirling with wild fervor, stirring the sea from its tranquil slumber as if a king were rousing his subjects to heed the call of adventure. The waters before them shimmered like a sea of gemstones in the fading twilight, each ripple catching the last rays of the sun, reflecting hues of gold, deep sapphire, and shimmering emerald.

With each incantation Leo uttered, the ocean began to respond, as if it were a sentient being, alive and aware of the hopes and fears of the sailors gathered at its edge. The surface of the water transformed into a living canvas, a brilliant display where the vibrant colors of hope collided with the shadows of despair, creating a breathtaking kaleidoscope that danced across the waves. This mesmerizing spectacle captured not just the eyes, but also the hearts of the sailors, igniting a fierce determination within them, ready to face whatever challenges lay ahead on their quest for the ocean's hidden treasures.

"Bring forth your strength and spirits, oh mighty seas!" Leo called out, his voice resonating with the cadence of the waves themselves, invoking the ancient powers that lay within the cold embrace of the ocean. The very air seemed to shimmer with his words, vibrating with an energy that coursed through the long-buried depths below. "Show us the way that leads back to our kin." His invocation transcended mere words; it was an appeal to the primordial forces of the deep, a summoning of the ocean's ancient wisdom to guide them toward safety and home.

With Leo at the helm, they ventured deeper into the heart of the ocean, leaving behind the familiar shores that had cradled them for so long. The fishermen, loyal and resolute, were tethered to his magic, their fates entwined with the very essence of the water that surrounded them. Each man brought his own hopes, fears, and dreams, blending into a tapestry of tenacity as they journeyed forward. The enticing whispers of the sea echoed around them—luring them with promises of endurance and salvation, beckoning with each swell of water beneath their small boat. Yet, as they drifted further into the murky unknown, dark clouds gathered ominously overhead, swirling with unsettling energy, a harbinger of the trials and tribulations that lay ahead.

The atmosphere shifted, thickening with a foreboding presence. The air grew heavy with tension, and Leo could feel the weight of the ocean's anger brewing, an invisible force that throbbed beneath the surface. The waves began to rise, towering like dark sentinels, preparing to test them against the formidable might of nature. Each surge and crash reverberated through the hull, a warning that echoed in the very marrow of their bones.

"What lies ahead?" one of the sailors murmured, his voice barely rising above the tumultuous sound of the churning waters that surrounded them. He cast a worried glance toward the horizon, where dark, roiling clouds coiled and twisted, their shapes ominous and menacing. Shadows danced across the water's surface, adding to the palpable sense of impending doom that hung in the air, a weight that pressed down upon their hearts like a leaden anchor.

"The embodiment of your fear," Leo replied, bravely steeling his heart against the encroaching tempest. He sensed the apprehension that coursed through his crewmates, their fears manifesting as shadows in their eyes. With a steadiness that belied the turmoil swirling within him, he turned to face the other sailors, his gaze piercing and unwavering. "To reclaim your ship and cement your fate, you must confront what you dread the most."

In that moment, Leo understood that they were not merely battling the elements; they were embarking on a journey of the spirit, a test that would uncover the hidden strength within each of them. The ocean was a living entity, a reflection of their innermost anxieties and desires. As they pressed forward, he knew that every swell and crash of the waves was a call to courage—a challenge to face the darkness, to emerge triumphant against the raging forces that sought to overwhelm them. With a renewed sense of purpose, the fishermen looked to their captain, drawing strength from his unwavering resolve, ready to embrace whatever lay ahead, come what may.

As the storm gathered strength on the horizon, the atmosphere thickened with an unsettling anticipation, conjuring a chilling sense of dread. The wind howled ferociously, its voice a shrill, mournful cry that echoed the despair brewing within the hearts of the sailors. Jagged forks of lightning danced across the turbulent sky, illuminating the scene with brief flashes that revealed the terrifying beauty of nature's fury. Against this backdrop of chaos, a colossal wave began to form, rising from the depths like some ancient sentinel of despair. Towering and menacing, it swelled with an immense power, a massive, watery harbinger ready to crash upon them and sweep them away into the abyss, threatening to engulf their very souls.

Leo stood at the bow of the ship, his heart pounding in sync with the tumultuous rhythm of the storm. He felt the heavy weight of anguish and regret seeping into his skin, saturating him with an overwhelming tide of emotions that felt deeper and more consuming than the turbulent sea itself. It was a profound sorrow that bound him to the other sailors, each of whom bore the invisible scars of loss. He could sense their collective despair, a palpable fog that laced the air with shadows of grief, suffocating their hopes for survival.

As memories of loss flickered through his mind like dying stars, struggling in the encroaching darkness, Leo realized how deeply intertwined they were with the daunting reality they now faced. Each face in the crew was a swirl of apprehension, a testament to their personal battles against the ghosts of those who had once sailed alongside them, their laughter now nothing more than echoes in the cruel maw of the sea.

"The wave of sorrow," Leo spoke softly, his voice barely rising above the roar of the tempest, almost as if he sought to reassure himself as much as those around him. "It stands before us as the haunting spirit of those lost at sea, tormenting the likes of you and me. But to chart our path forward, we must confront it together."

As they drew nearer to the malevolent wave, its monstrous form loomed larger, and the air crackled with charged electricity, amplifying the sense of foreboding that draped over the crew like a heavy cloak. An eerie silence settled momentarily as they faced this titan of water, during which Leo could feel the fear clamoring within each sailor's heart. They huddled together, seeking comfort in their shared vulnerability, their faces reflecting a harrowing mix of trepidation and despair that seemed to mirror the roiling sea.

Yet, amidst the chaos, a profound sense of resolution surged within Leo, an unyielding determination that he could not ignore. In that moment, he recognized that they could not simply succumb to their fears; they must stand firm against the tide of anxiety threatening to overwhelm them. "Stand with your fears or they will consume you," Leo urged, his voice rising above the furious wind that sought to carry away his words. "Remember those you lost; remember their strength and resilience. It is this love, this unwavering memory that will guide you through the darkness."

With each word, he infused courage into the hearts of his fellow sailors, transforming apprehension into a collective resolve. They glanced at one another, a silent understanding passing between them, as the flickering light of hope ignited within their souls. Together, they braced for the impending storm, ready to battle not only the monstrous wave before them but also the shadows of grief that trailed in its wake. It was then, united in purpose and memory, that they dared to hope—for themselves and for those they had loved and lost.

In a bold act of defiance against the oppressive despair that sought to engulf them, Leo summoned every ounce of his latent power, channeling the vibrant energy born from the sailors' shared memories. He closed his eyes and began to envision a myriad of moments—the carefree laughter of crew members as they splashed playfully about the deck during sunny, calm days when the sea was like glass, reflecting the endless blue sky above. He recalled the palpable joy that filled their hearts upon returning to port after enduring a long and arduous journey, the weary yet triumphant hugs exchanged, and the exuberant shouts of celebration as they reunited with loved ones.

He felt the warmth of memories reminding him of the unbreakable camaraderie that had been forged in the midst of fierce storms, bonds as sturdy and resilient as the hull of their beloved ship, which had weathered so many tempests alongside them. This profound connection between the sailors formed an invisible thread that tied them together in that moment. As Leo focused deeply, the energy began to ignite around them, swirling like a vibrant whirlwind infused with life and spirit. It wove together their collective histories, crafting a magnificent tapestry of memories that enveloped them in a warm and protective glow, a shield against the encroaching darkness.

Amidst all this, a colossal wave surged menacingly toward them, towering like a dark shadow that threatened to swallow them whole in a single, merciless gulp. But as they stood together, unified in spirit and purpose, drawing forth the immense strength of their collective memories, the wave trembled before them. It quivered, as if sensing the potent force of their unwavering resilience and hope. A brilliant light began to radiate from their intertwined connection, slicing through the oppressive darkness that loomed above them like a thick fog.

Then, in a moment that felt almost otherworldly, as the titanic wave crashed down upon them, a miraculous phenomenon occurred—it parted in two, as though the very fabric of reality had bent to their united will. They sailed through the chasm, a narrow path created amidst the chaos, emerging on the other side. Unscathed and buoyant, they were filled with renewed hope, their hearts uplifted, as they realized that no darkness could ever extinguish the light of their shared bonds and memories. They were not just individual sailors but rather a living testament to the strength of unity, ready to face whatever challenges lay ahead, buoyed by the glory of their unbreakable spirit.

With renewed vigor and an electrifying sense of purpose coursing through their veins, the sailors finally spotted the long-lost outline of the Dawnstar, marooned and ghostly against the backdrop of the darkened sea. The ship loomed like a haunting specter, its once-magnificent sails tattered and faded, a mere shadow of the proud vessel it had once been amidst the grand voyages of yesteryear. As Leo, at the helm, skillfully steered the sailors closer, an almost reverent silence enveloped the crew, each one captivated by the solemn sight before them.

"Together," Leo urged, his eyes blazing with a fierce glint of determination and unwavering resolve, "we can restore her. Together, we will make her whole again." His voice rang out like a clarion call, igniting an ember of hope within the hearts of his crew, each man and woman standing shoulder to shoulder, united in this shared dream of revival.

Harnessing the raw, untamed forces of the elements, Leo began to channel the sailors' heartfelt prayers and intentions into the waters surrounding the vessel. As if orchestrating a symphony of energy, he focused their collective strength, weaving it into a tapestry of light that began to ripple beneath the surface. Soon, a golden luminescence shimmered up from the depths, a radiant glow that wrapped around the ship like a long-lost embrace, cradling her in a cocoon of hope and renewal.

The warmth of the light pulsed with life, as if the very essence of the seawater was responding to their devotion, healing the weathered wood and frayed rigging with each gentle lap of the undulating sea. The Dawnstar, once the pride of the fleet, began to creak and groan, awakening from a deep slumber as splintered masts slowly began to straighten and realign, each movement a testament to the collective will of the sailors who yearned for her revival.

As the cheers erupted joyously from the crew, the ship's transformation unfolded before their eyes. It was a sight to behold: her form regained and her full glory returning like the dazzling sunrise after a long, moonlit night beneath the haunting lullabies of the ocean. The sailors embraced one another fervently, tears of gratitude streaming down their cheeks, mingling with gales of laughter. Their joy burst forth like the final rays of a dying sun, illuminating the horizon with hopes rekindled and dreams reborn in the vibrant light of a new day.

"You've done the impossible!" the burly sailor exclaimed, his voice filled with awe and disbelief. Tears of joy began to pool in his eyes, glistening like dew drops in the early morning light as he looked at Leo, marveling at the extraordinary transformation that had taken place before their very eyes. The change was not just in the ship, but in their spirits, their hopes, and their very understanding of what they could achieve together.

"We did it together!" Leo replied, beaming with pride and joy, a big grin stretching across his face. He was fully aware that it was their deepening bonds of friendship and unity—their unwavering faith in one another—that had carried them through the most significant challenge they had ever faced. Each setback had only seemed to strengthen their resolve, and in that moment, their shared triumph was a testament to the power of camaraderie.

As dawn broke over the horizon, spilling streams of golden light across the glistening surface of the sea, Leo felt an exhilarating rush of victory coursing through him, almost palpable in the cool, salty air. The ocean's majestic voice seemed to echo around them, filled with enticing promises of exploration, adventure, and uncharted territories just waiting to be discovered. It was a powerful reminder of their duty to protect those who dared to venture upon its treacherous depths.

With a final bow of gratitude towards the dawn that welcomed them, the sailors and Leo set sail atop the revitalized Dawnstar, their beloved ship that now seemed more alive than ever before. They left behind not just the physical remnants of their struggles but also waves of exuberance and a myriad of sorrows that had been transformed into sources of immense strength. Each wave behind them served as a reminder of what they had overcome and the new horizons that awaited them.

As Leo stood upon the shore, watching the magnificent ship slice through the water, he felt an indelible connection bind him to the sea. The salt in the air and the rhythmic lapping of the waves against the hull seemed to whisper secrets only he could hear. This bond would serve as an eternal reminder that in the face of great challenges and adversity, the true worth of the heart lies not in individual accomplishments, but in the ties that bind us together. It was these connections—the friendships forged under duress, the shared laughter, the support in times of despair—that he realized were his greatest treasure of all.

Chapter 6

The sun had barely begun to peek over the horizon, casting a pale golden hue that struggled to pierce through a thick blanket of brooding clouds, when Leo made his fateful decision—one that held the weight of the day ahead, and perhaps the very lives of many who called this coastal town home. The sky was transformed into a tapestry of dark chaos, with swirling shadows comprised of tumultuous greys and blacks, looming heavily as though the heavens themselves were in mourning. The wind howled ferociously through the sails of the small fishing vessel they had boarded, its voice rising and falling like a restless spirit yearning for solace. This was no ordinary day at sea; an urgent call to action reverberated in the salty air, wrapping itself around Leo like an invisible shroud.

The townsfolk's hushed conversations—barely more than whispers that crept through the salty breeze—echoed painfully in his mind. Fishermen, brave men who had ventured into the churning waves just the evening before, had not returned, leaving only the specter of concern and an unsettling silence in their absence. They were lost, it seemed, ensnared in the belly of a tempest that threatened to swallow the horizon whole, leaving behind an emptiness that tugged sharply at Leo's heartstrings, awakening a growing sense of dread that nestled in the pit of his stomach.

As Leo cast his eyes across the deck at his crew, a palpable sense of determination etched across their weathered faces mirrored his own unyielding conviction. Each sailor had their motivations for braving the unpredictable and turbulent seas—some were brothers, bound by blood and shared history, some were devoted fathers, their concern for their families driving them to take risks no matter the danger, and others were mere friends, connected through years of shared dreams and heartfelt hardships. They placed their unwavering trust in Leo, not merely as their captain, but as a man who possessed an unusual and almost mystical affinity for the sea—a rare talent he had meticulously honed over many years, learning to listen to the whispers of the waters and interpret its hidden language. He was not just a skilled mariner; he was nearly one with the ocean, capable of understanding its moods and subtle cues in ways few others could.

"Steady!" Leo commanded, his voice slicing through the tempestuous gusts with an authority that inspired immediate action. The crew sprang into motion, their hands moving with the precision and synchrony of well-oiled machinery, each sailor fulfilling a crucial role in the collective effort to ready the sturdy vessel for the impending squall that loomed ominously ahead. They secured themselves to the deck, ropes binding them firmly in place as the salty spray of the ocean misted against their skin, revitalizing their spirits with the bracing touch of the sea. The weight of impending danger hung thick in the air, but it only fueled their determination.

Leo stood resolute at the helm, a bastion of steadiness against the encroaching chaos, feeling the anticipation of the storm swirl within him like a whirlpool—both electrifying and daunting. The depths of the ocean pulsed beneath his feet, its rhythms harmonizing delightfully with the steady beat of his own heart. The surrounding pandemonium—the howling winds and crashing waves—began to feel like a dialogue, an old conversation echoing between man and nature, whispering promises of challenge and adventure. He was prepared to respond, to assert his will against the tumultuous forces that threatened to overwhelm them.

With determination igniting his very core, Leo closed his eyes, seeking to center himself amidst the maelstrom closing in around him. His hands outstretched before him, fingers twitching with the intent of a maestro conducting a mighty symphony, he reached out toward the churning waters, hoping to connect to the pulse of the sea itself. The energy within him surged like a tidal wave, a warm glow rising from the depths of his being, radiating through his arms and reaching out into the tempestuous atmosphere around him. With a gentle flick of his wrist, he called upon the depths of the great sea, yearning for a sense of harmony amidst its chaotic dance.

At first, seemingly nothing happened. The waves continued their violent ballet, crashing mercilessly against the hull and vehemently resisting his efforts. But Leo was undeterred, refusing to yield to despair or the suffocating grip of anxiety. He dug deeper within himself, anchoring his spirit to the profound, ancient connection he felt with the waters surrounding him. "Calm," he whispered, the single word infused with a potency borne of deep faith and desperate hope. "Return to peace." He poured every ounce of his being into that invocation, willing it to resonate with the very soul of the storm itself, hoping to mend the rift between their raw natures and restore balance to the tempest.

At that moment, a profound hush settled over him, an almost sacred silence that enveloped the chaos around him, as if the very storm paused to consider his plea. It was as if time itself held its breath, allowing the weight of the world to drift momentarily away. Then, like the miraculous answer to a desperate prayer, the cacophony of wind and waves began to quiet. Leo felt a deep sense of connection, as though he had plucked a single string in an expansive orchestra filled with the harmonious interplay of nature. Each ripple of serenity emanated from that note, spreading across the turbulent surface of the sea like a soothing balm.

The wind, which had howled fiercely before, began to slow its relentless assault, transforming into a gentle breeze that caressed the ship. The waves, once monstrous and unforgiving, started to soften, their tumultuous roar fading into a calming whisper. Leo's crew, who had been clinging to their posts and battling the storm's fury with determined grit, now stared in awe as the ship began to steady itself. They could sense the shift—the vessel was no longer at the mercy of the violent pull of nature, but rather, it was being gently nudged by the calm he had summoned, a transformation that filled them with renewed hope.

"Look!" one sailor shouted, his voice rising above the stillness, eyes wide with astonishment as he pointed toward the horizon. There, just beyond the tumultuous shroud of the storm, a flicker of lights danced amidst the lingering shadows—a distress signal from a vessel far off in the distance, a beacon of hope piercing through the darkness. The sight was surreal, igniting a spark of determination within them.

"We've got to help them!" another crew member urged, the urgency in his voice laced with adrenaline, the excitement palpable in the damp air that clung to their skin. His words sent a ripple of action through the crew, a tangible shift in energy as they began to rally towards the challenge that lay ahead.

Leo's heart sank at the sight. It was the second fishing vessel from their town—the very one he had dreaded might have succumbed to the storm's merciless grip, lost to the chaotic sea. Against the swirling backdrop of his emotions, he quickly turned the ship toward the glimmering lights, his focus sharpening with the weight of responsibility. He could see the determination in his crew's eyes, recognizing that they were not just fighting for their own survival, but for those on that distant vessel, perhaps fighting for their lives.

He felt the storm's impact, the toll it had taken evident in the churning sea that roared around them, a stark testament to its fury. Yet in that moment, as his heart raced and resolve surged through him, he realized they still had a fighting chance. With the spirit of the ocean at his command and his crew steadfastly behind him, united by a shared purpose, Leo prepared to forge ahead into the unknown. He steeled himself for the daunting task that lay ahead, ready to face whatever challenges awaited them, embracing the daunting responsibility—and the flicker of hope—that shone on the horizon.

They navigated through the lessened waves, the air thick with tension and resolve—a palpable mix of adrenaline and fear swirling around them like the ocean spray. The horizon shimmered beneath a muted sun, casting hues of gold and grey across the tumultuous sea, as if the very sky itself was mirroring the turmoil below. Each swell of the water seemed to echo with unspoken challenges, as the ship forged its way toward the beleaguered vessel wrestling against the currents that threatened to swallow it whole.

At the helm, Leo stood tall, a beacon of unwavering determination amidst the chaos. His presence commanded the ship with a blend of authority and grace, the very embodiment of courage in the face of uncertainty. He held his stance firm and resolute against the backdrop of crashing waves, every muscle in his body attuned to the rhythm of the ocean, ready to respond to the unpredictable nature of their surroundings.

The distressed boat bobbed precariously in the restless waters, barely afloat, a chaotic assemblage of splintered wood and strained rigging that screamed of its struggles. Each rise and fall of the hull echoed the desperation of its crew, men and women who had fought valiantly against the merciless tide, now trapped in a battle for their very survival. The sailors aboard the troubled craft waved their arms frantically, their faces pale with trepidation and fear—a haunting sight that stirred deep emotions within Leo's heart, igniting a fire of empathy and purpose within him.

Unfazed by the turmoil around him, Leo inhaled deeply, grounding himself, taking a moment to stabilize his nerves and focus his mind on the task at hand. "We're coming!" he called out, the firmness in his voice cutting through the howling wind like a beacon of hope piercing through the ominous clouds. His words carried a promise, a pledge of rescue that reverberated across the churning water, instilling a sense of courage in those who heard him.

As they closed the distance, the stronger waves that had previously held them at bay began to reform, cresting higher with a renewed vigor in their pursuit, as if seeking to thwart Leo's mission. Yet, with Leo's unwavering guidance steering them onward, the crew rallied around him with a fierce determination. The urgency of their situation ignited a sense of camaraderie among them, their spirits lifted by the conviction that radiated from their leader.

With every passing moment, they worked tirelessly, throwing lines and securing their own vessel with a fervor born not only of desperation but also of an unyielding sense of duty. "Catch this!" Leo shouted, his voice firm and clear as he tossed a sturdy rope toward the sinking ship, his eyes locked onto the panicked faces of the hunters of the sea—individuals who, just like him, had once ventured forth with dreams and ambitions, now caught in the snare of the merciless waves.

The rope soared through the air, its path a lifeline between despair and hope, and with it came a surge of determination that bridged the chasm of fear, reinforcing the resolve of both crews in a desperate bid for survival. Leo's heart raced as he watched, holding his breath as time seemed to stretch like the taut lines of their rigging, waiting for either the embrace of safety or the cruel embrace of the ocean's depths, knowing full well that every soul battled their own demons in this tempestuous moment.

One by one, lanterns flickered to life amidst the chaos, their soft illumination cutting through the darkness like a lifeline. The warm glow enveloped the astonished expressions of the stranded crew, their eyes wide with disbelief and gratitude as they grasped the lifelines of salvation with trembling hands. Each lantern's light seemed to whisper promises of hope, reviving the spirits of those who had faced the ocean's wrath and survived its treachery.

The first to respond was an older fisherman named Calder, a rugged man with a face etched by the brine and wind, his weathered skin a testament to the countless years he had spent braving the ocean's capricious nature. It bore the marks of storms weathered and dangers navigated, wisdom accumulated through lifetimes spent on the restless seas. With a surge of effort born from instinct and desperation, he swung himself onto their craft, landing with a thud that momentarily silenced the tumult around him. The relief was palpable in the air, a collective exhalation as he landed, breathless but standing, his frame a pillar of resilience amidst the swirling turmoil.

"Hurry! We have to get everyone aboard!" he exclaimed, his voice a tempestuous mix of relief and urgent command, each word resonating with a gravity that demanded immediate action. His eyes, sharp and alert, darted back toward his beleaguered comrades still clinging to the doomed vessel, their silhouettes stark against the night sky—a poignant reminder of the peril they all faced.

With resilience fueling their movements and a sense of purpose igniting their souls, Leo and his dedicated team quickly moved into action. They worked with a fervor that belied their own fatigue, hands reaching out to pull in the remaining fishermen one by one. Each man grasped onto the safety lines as if their very lives depended on it; in truth, they did. Exhaustion painted their faces, the shadows of weariness looming beneath their brows like storm clouds drifting overhead. Yet amidst the fatigue, a spark of victory glimmered brightly in their eyes, igniting determination to forge ahead, to rescue their brothers from the jaws of despair.

With every passing moment, they moved in synchrony, the rhythm of their actions underscored by the pounding of their hearts. Adrenaline surged through their veins, propelling them forward as they continued to bring their comrades aboard. Finally, the last crew member, a youthful lad barely out of his teens with wide, fearful eyes, was hoisted over the edge and onto the deck. He landed heavily, collapsing onto the worn planks that had borne witness to the trials of many. With a gasp of relief, he curled into himself, grateful to have escaped the clutches of the unforgiving sea, their collective triumph echoing in the quiet aftermath of the storm. Together, they formed an unbreakable bond, united by their harrowing experience and the flickering lanterns that now illuminated the path to safety and hope.

Once they were all aboard, Leo took a moment to survey his ship and the crew that stood beside him on the deck. The sight of them stirred something deep within him, a complex mixture of emotions that swirled like the ocean itself. They were worn and wind-tossed, bearing the marks of their arduous journey etched on their faces and bodies; every drop of saltwater that clung to them was a reminder of the harrowing trials they had faced together. Wind-burnt and weary, they bore the scars of their battles against nature's fury. Yet, amidst the weariness and tumult of their recent ordeal, he couldn't help but feel a sense of pride swell within his chest like the breaking waves. They had not just survived; they had triumphed against the odds, facing the ravenous tempest and emerging victorious. With every heartbeat, they could feel the bond of camaraderie growing stronger amidst the aftermath of chaos, forged not just by the ordeal they had endured but also by the unwavering spirit of hope and resilience that surged through them like a scorching flame, brightening the shadows of doubt that hung heavy over their thoughts.

"Back to shore!" Leo commanded, his voice ringing out with a fervor that ignited the spirits of his crew, rejuvenating their weary hearts and dull spirits. His words cut through the remnants of the storm like a beacon guiding them home. The intensity of his passion pulsed through the air, weaving a vibrant tapestry of determination that enveloped them all, setting the course for their journey ahead. Together, as one cohesive unit, they manoeuvred through the remnants of the storm that had raged like an untamed beast just moments before, their movements synchronized as if they were a single entity. The fierce winds, which had once whipped mercilessly at their faces with icy fingers and rattled their vessel like a plaything in a child's hands, began to surrender to the calm that they had collectively created through sheer willpower, teamwork, and an unyielding sense of purpose. They harnessed the strength of their collective spirit, leaning into the challenge and channeling their energy into navigating the turbulent waters that still swirled around them, guiding their ship toward safety.

By the time they reached the harbor, the sky had transformed into a breathtaking canvas, painted with radiant strokes of orange and gold. The hues cast a serene glow over the landscape, standing in stark contrast to the peril they had just braved. It was as if the very universe itself was celebrating their safe return, wrapping the scene in an embrace of warmth and light, acknowledging their struggle and endurance against the formidable forces of nature. The townsfolk, who had been anxiously awaiting their return, had gathered at the docks, their expressions a mixture of disbelief and overwhelming gratitude as they witnessed the emergence of Leo and his courageous crew from the storm's wrath. There was a palpable sense of relief and joy among them, as if the very air vibrated with an electric energy of hope rekindled. Cheers erupted from the crowd as they hailed their heroes, their voices merging into a symphony of praise that echoed around the harbor, amplifying the sense of triumph that hung in the air.

As Leo stepped onto the dock, the cheers of the crowd enveloped him like a warm blanket, wrapping him in an embrace of shared joy and relief that resonated deeply within his soul. The cacophony of exuberant voices swelled around him, creating a joyful symphony that completely drowned out the lingering echoes of fear that had haunted him during the ordeal. Each cheer that erupted from the crowd felt like an affirmation, an uplifting wave that momentarily lifted the weight of fatigue threatening to anchor his spirit in despair. The rescue was complete; lives had been saved, futures preserved, and in that electrifying moment—surrounded by cheers and laughter—Leo understood the true potential and magnitude of his extraordinary gift. It was a power not just meant for weathering the physical storms that churned menacingly in the skies above, but also for bringing radiant hope and a sense of purpose to those who found themselves adrift in the turbulent waters of despair.

As the sun dipped gracefully below the horizon, casting long shadows that danced along the wooden planks of the dock, it ignited the vast expanse of the sea with a myriad of shimmering reflections, each one glimmering with the colors of hope. Leo found himself gazing back out towards the infinite vastness of the ocean, reflecting on its untamed beauty and fierce unpredictability. He knew all too well that the storms would inevitably return, unpredictable and fierce as ever, clawing at the serenity of the waters. Yet even amid this understanding, he felt reassured and resolute. The preparation he had committed to, the countless hours spent training with his loyal crew, had equipped him to face whatever nature threw at them. Together, they stood as a formidable team, steadfast and united, ready to confront the challenges that lay ahead.

The gentle whispers of the ocean, both soothing and fierce, would forever guide him home—a silent promise that the strength of their shared journey would light the way through even the darkest of waters. In that moment, as Leo stood there feeling the cool evening breeze against his skin, he experienced a renewed sense of purpose swell within him. A stirring commitment blossomed in his heart, one that urged him to brave the coming storms with unwavering courage and resourcefulness, ready to embrace any challenges that lay ahead. As his gaze lingered on the horizon, Leo felt a fire ignite within him, a determination to harness his gifts not just to protect himself or his crew but to be a beacon of hope to all those who found themselves lost in the tempestuous sea of uncertainty. With a deep breath, he prepared to navigate whatever trials awaited, fueled by his unshakeable belief in the power of resilience and the unbreakable bonds of camaraderie.

Chapter 7

The warm glow of the setting sun bathed the sleepy harbor town in a golden light, creating a scene that felt almost otherworldly, as if it had been painted by the brush of a master artist. The gentle hues of amber and rose softened the rugged features of the quaint cottages that lined the water's edge, giving them a dreamlike quality. Each cottage, with its weathered wood and vibrant window boxes brimming with late-blooming flowers, seemed to sway gently in rhythm with the old ships that bobbed peacefully in the tranquil water. Long shadows stretched across the cobblestone streets, a fleeting reminder of day's end as the sun sank lower on the horizon.

In the distance, the melodic chime of a bell echoed through the air, announcing the hour with a familiar cadence that resonated with the heartbeat of the village. This harmonious sound melded seamlessly with the joyful shouts of laughter and cheers erupting along the pier as villagers eagerly awaited the sailors' return. They filled the air with bright energy—faces illuminated by the soft, fading light of the sun—gathering in clusters to exchange stories and share in the anticipation of the homecoming. For the townsfolk, this was not merely a ritual of greeting; it represented the revival of hope after enduring the long, grim chapter of uncertainty brought about by the sailors' absence. Each reunion was steeped in longing, relief, and an unspoken bond that tied the community together, a collective sigh of release at the thought of loved ones eventually returning from the treacherous waters.

Yet, in the midst of this bustling scene, one name stood out—Leo. This young man, often overlooked and underestimated due to his unassuming demeanor, had unexpectedly emerged as the unsung hero of the day. While others reveled in joyous embraces, Leo had proven himself through an act of extraordinary bravery. Amidst the chaos of tumultuous waves and raging storms, his keen sense of navigation and unwavering courage had guided the beleaguered sailors away from what could have been their watery graves, pulling them from the ocean's deep, unforgiving grip.

As the sailors finally docked their battered vessel, each face was alight with joy, their expressions bubbling over with stories of survival and adventure even before a single word was spoken. The crew worked quickly, throwing ropes over the weathered mooring posts, the familiar motions a mix of relief and urgency, as if the simple act of securing their ship would tether their souls back to safety. The townsfolk surged forward, a wave of ecstatic humanity flooding the pier, clapping, shouting, and celebrating this long-awaited reunion.

Amidst the exuberant throng, Leo remained slightly apart, a quiet observer of the chaotic yet heartwarming scene. An overwhelming mix of humility and awkwardness washed over him as he absorbed the vibrant celebrations surrounding him. The wild joy that swirled in the air felt almost surreal, and he couldn't quite shake the indelible feeling of disbelief that washed over him—he had once again managed to rise to the occasion when hope had flickered so dimly.

Suddenly, a burly sailor named Jirn broke through the jubilant crowd, making his way toward Leo with a determined stride that exuded unrestrained gratitude and affection. Without hesitation, he swept Leo into a bear hug that nearly knocked the breath from his lungs. The sheer force of Jirn's embrace elicited laughter from those nearby, a moment of levity amid the emotional fervor. "By the sea gods, you saved us!" Jirn exclaimed, his voice booming, filled with a depth of feeling that resonated with everyone around. "I can't thank you enough!"

Another sailor, Mira, whose spirit sparkled with enthusiasm, chimed in, her eyes gleaming like stars in the twilight sky. "We're alive because of you, Leo! All those nights on the storm-tossed seas, we thought—" Her words trailed off, laden with the weight of their shared fears, but Jirn, ever the steadfast companion, cut in, his resolve ringing clear. "But we came back," he stated firmly, glancing at Leo with reverence. "And it's all thanks to you."

As the sailors began to gather, sharing harrowing tales of terror and triumph, a palpable sense of camaraderie enveloped them. They recounted their desperate struggle against nature's wrath, of how despair had threatened to overtake them until Leo had emerged as a beacon of hope—a guiding light in the storm. The captivated villagers, drawn closer by the magnetic energy that filled the air, listened intently, their faces reflecting a newfound admiration and respect for the young man who had risked everything, standing brave and resolute against the odds to save those lost in the storm. Each story woven into the fabric of that evening became a tribute to Leo's courage—an ode not just to survival but to the profound strength found in the bonds of community and the heroism that can often be found in the most unexpected places.

The warm glow of the setting sun bathed the sleepy harbor town in a golden light, casting an enchanting spell that transformed the mundane into the extraordinary. The horizon blazed with hues of orange and pink, as if nature itself were celebrating the day's conclusion. This celestial display infused the atmosphere with an almost ethereal quality, creating a dreamlike ambiance that felt both familiar and otherworldly.

The soft rays of sunlight enveloped the rustic cottages that adorned the waterfront, their rugged features softened by the warm illumination. Each cottage, with its weathered stone and painted wooden shutters, seemed to take on a new life beneath the sun's tender caress, while the long shadows of the old ships grazed the tranquil surface of the water, rippling gently like whispers of a forgotten era. The faint sound of water lapping against the hulls created an almost melodic backdrop, harmonizing with the distant chime of a bell that celebrated the hour, its tones echoing across the harbor and mingling with the sounds of laughter and cheers that erupted along the bustling pier.

Villagers, faces aglow with the radiant light of the setting sun, gathered in eager anticipation to welcome the sailors back to shore. Each person stood on the verge of excitement, their hearts swelling with joy, as they prepared to embrace familiar faces returning home after enduring weeks adrift in the tempestuous seas. The reunion represented far more than just a greeting; it signified the end of a grim chapter filled with worry and despair that had cast a lingering shadow over their lives—a collective sigh of relief resonating among them as the tension of the past few weeks began to dissipate.

Amidst this sea of jubilant reunions and heartfelt embraces stood one figure—Leo. This unassuming young man, often overlooked and underestimated by many, had emerged as a beacon of heroism in their time of peril. Through an extraordinary act of bravery during their harrowing ordeal, he had defied the odds, showcasing astute navigation skills and unwavering fortitude that ultimately pulled the beleaguered crew from the merciless jaws of the ocean's depths.

As the sailors expertly docked their battered vessel, a palpable sense of joy illuminated their faces, transforming their weathered countenances into vibrant portraits of relief and triumph. The crew hastily threw ropes over the enduring mooring posts with a sense of urgency, securing their ship with a mix of relief and palpable excitement. The townsfolk surged forward, fueled by an electrifying current of emotions, much like a river bursting its banks—clapping, shouting, and celebrating this long-awaited reunion with wild abandon.

Among the exuberant crowd, Leo found himself standing a little apart, a quiet observer of the chaotic yet heartwarming scene unfolding around him. A combination of humility and awkwardness washed over him as he watched the joyous atmosphere swirl like confetti in the air. The heady mix of elation and disbelief filled him, leaving him momentarily awestruck that he had once again risen to an occasion that seemed insurmountable when all hope appeared lost.

In that moment of introspection, a burly sailor named Jirn broke through the throng with a determined stride, charging towards Leo as if propelled by the very winds of fate itself. Without warning, he enveloped Leo in an overwhelming bear hug that nearly knocked the breath from his lungs, causing laughter to erupt from those around them like the joyous peal of bells. "By the sea gods, you saved us!" Jirn exclaimed, his voice booming with raw emotion, filled with heart-felt gratitude. "I can't thank you enough!"

Another sailor, Mira, quickly joined in, her lively spirit shining through as she chimed in enthusiastically. Her eyes sparkled like distant stars in the burgeoning twilight. "We're alive because of you! All those nights on the storm-tossed seas, we thought it was the end—"

"But we came back," Jirn interrupted, his voice ringing with a sense of resolute purpose, a proud declaration that underscored the gravity of their experiences. "And it's all thanks to you, Leo."

As the buoyant sailors began to share their harrowing tales of terror and triumph, each story painted a vivid picture of their desperate struggle against nature's fury. They recounted the moments when hope had nearly slipped from their grasp, how despair loomed large in the raging waters, and how it was Leo who emerged when all seemed lost—a guiding light radiating wisdom and bravery that steadied their hearts amid the chaos. The captivated villagers listened with rapt attention, their faces reflecting a newfound admiration and respect for the young man who had risked his own safety to save those lost in the storm, a hero born from the depths of fear yet shining with boundless courage. In that movie-like atmosphere of unity, Leo's heart swelled, not from ego, but with the warmth of the community that now recognized the strength within their own.

"Let's prepare a feast!" shouted Mira, her face aglow with anticipation, the words spilling out like a bubbling brook, flowing with an infectious energy that rippled through the gathering. She clapped her hands together, and that simple gesture seemed to ignite a spark of enthusiasm within the crowd, illuminating their spirits as if the sun had emerged from behind a cloud. "The tavern will ring with laughter and song! We'll tell tales of the waves and toast to our brave Leo!"

Her proclamation was like the striking of a match in a quiet room, immediately capturing the attention of everyone present. With those words, the atmosphere metamorphosed, charged with a newfound sense of purpose and euphoria. The townsfolk, once leisurely leaning against the weathered posts of the harbour, sprang into action, their hearts swelling with a shared excitement as they began to brainstorm and plan an unforgettable celebration. Whispers of potential dishes floated through the air—aromatic stews, succulent roasted meats, and pies filled with the ripest fruits of the season—while merry discussions erupted around them like fireworks, each idea sparking laughter and joy. The air itself seemed to pulsate with the exhilarating thought of what stories would be shared under the soft glow of lanterns, their light mingling with the embers of gratitude and camaraderie that Leo had sparked within their hearts.

In the midst of this vibrant chaos, Leo stood, feeling a surge of warmth enveloping him like a comforting blanket. No longer was he simply a quiet observer of the life that thrived in the sleepy harbour town; for the first time, he felt an essential part of this lively tapestry, intricately woven together by threads of shared experience, loyalty, and newfound respect. Each cheer and cheer echoed in his heart, reflecting the strength of community that surrounded him.

Thus, the decision to celebrate was forged, strengthened by the animated debate and joyful banter that had unfolded among the villagers. After lengthy discussions garnished with laughter and fervent nods of agreement, a collective sentiment surfaced—a fervent consensus that made their hearts race with glee. With a shared purpose, the villagers darted off in every conceivable direction, their enthusiasm infectious and bright, igniting the harbour with a sense of jubilation akin to a dazzling fireworks display lighting up the sky on a clear night.

The festive preparations quickly transformed the air around them into a medley of enticing aromas. The enticing fragrance of meats roasting over open flames danced through the air, its rich, smoky scent curling delightfully into the evening sky, mingling with the sweet, warm odor of freshly baked bread wafting from the village ovens. This fragrant concoction drew together a community united by culinary delights, intertwining beautifully with the invigorating scent of sea salt. It was a comforting reminder of the vast ocean hugging their quaint home, its rhythms and tides as familiar to them as the laughter shared between neighbours.

As dusk settled majestically over the horizon, lanterns flickered to life like tiny stars newly sprung from the earth, their soft, golden glow illuminating the cobblestone streets with a tender embrace. Laughter rang out like melodious bells, harmonizing effortlessly with the gentle lap of the waves against the harbour, melding together to create a symphony of joy that filled the warm evening air. Children dashed about near the water's edge, their delighted squeals punctuating the atmosphere with carefree glee, while the village elders exchanged knowing smiles enriched with wisdom, reminiscing about the golden days woven into the fabric of their shared history.

When the villagers finally gathered at the tavern, a beloved central hub of camaraderie and hearty celebration, the collective atmosphere brimmed with gratitude and the sweet essence of hope. Leo found himself seated at the head of a long, polished wooden table, its surface worn smooth through countless gatherings and the numerous stories told over the years. Surrounded by a lively motley crew of sailors—seasoned travelers whose eyes sparkled with unspent adventure—he was enraptured by their thrilling escapades. Their animated voices intertwined, creating an orchestra of tales that whisked him away to distant lands kissed by shimmering sunlight and dangerous waters that had tested their mettle.

With each story shared, images of fairy-tale realms glimmered just beyond the horizon, where exotic creatures drifted gracefully through azure depths, and formidable storms rose to challenge the resolve of even the bravest hearts. He listened intently, captivated by the tales of the sea's treachery and beauty, as the atmosphere knit itself tighter with every laugh, every cheer, and every shared memory, weaving Leo into the very soul of the community that had so fervently embraced him. This night, filled with laughter and song, would forever stand as a testament to the bonds forged in the heart of their beloved harbour town.

Amidst the clinking of mugs filled with frothy ale and the joyous chorus of animated conversations that filled the air with a vibrant energy, Jirn, a well-respected elder with a voice that demanded attention and carried the weight of authority, rose to his feet. He raised his cup high above his head, allowing the flickering candlelight to catch the gleam of the vessel and reflect the enthusiasm of the moment. "To our saviour! May his courage echo through our tales for generations to come!" he proclaimed with heartfelt sincerity, his voice resonating with deep emotion, each word infused with the weight of gratitude and reverence.

The room fell momentarily silent, each villager hanging on Jirn's words, feeling the importance of the moment. Then, as if ignited by a collective spark, the crowd erupted in an enthusiastic chorus. "To Leo!" they cheered, their voices rising to a powerful crescendo that reverberated off the wooden beams of the tavern, melding into a powerful anthem of gratitude. The joyful sound wrapped around Leo like a warm blanket, enveloping his heart in an overwhelming mix of warmth and humility. It was not merely a cheer; it transcended the ordinary to become a resounding promise of remembrance. It was a pledge, a vow that they would carry forth the legacy of bravery and selflessness that Leo had so boldly embodied during his time of trial.

In that defining moment, surrounded by a sea of smiling faces, laughter, and the clinking of mugs, Leo felt a profound sense of belonging that went beyond mere friendship. He realized that these people, gathered in celebration, were not just neighbors but family. They were bound together in a tapestry woven from shared experiences, trials, and triumphs, a community united in their spirits and hearts. As the joyous celebration continued to reverberate in the air with music, laughter, and animated stories of past adventures, Leo looked around at the familiar faces that had supported him throughout his journey. He knew, in the depths of his being, that he had forged an unbreakable bond with the villagers—one that would stand the test of time, fortified by their collective memories and experiences.

He felt the warmth of their appreciation envelop him entirely, wrapping him in a comforting cocoon that shielded him from past doubts and uncertainties. This feeling was profound, almost like being held in a nurturing embrace, where every ounce of skepticism that once lingered in his mind was gently washed away. It was a moment suspended in time, not merely a celebration of his recent victories; it signified a transformative awakening for both him and the villagers who had, until now, eyed him with a mix of scepticism and wariness. Their gazes, once filled with doubt and suspicion, now sparkled with admiration and acceptance; he could see it in their smiles, the way they clapped him on the back and greeted him with open arms, hailing him as one of their own—a deserving member of their community, someone who had earned their trust and camaraderie through sheer determination and courage.

In that vibrant atmosphere, amidst the laughter and the joyous chatter that danced through the air, it dawned on him just then that true bravery stemmed not only from performing extraordinary feats under great duress but also from the quiet strength required to foster connections, nurture relationships, and embrace the unlikeliest of allies along the journey of life. As he reflected on the trials he had faced, he began to understand that his path to heroism was not solely marked by triumphant moments of valor, but rather by the acts of kindness and empathy exchanged between him and the villagers. It was this shared humanity that had woven the threads of their community together, stronger and more resilient, reinforcing the bonds that they had cultivated over time.

As the night wore on, the sounds of the sea mingled with bursts of laughter, creating a symphony that echoed the heartbeats of those gathered. The rhythmic crash of the waves in the distance seemed to harmonize with the heartfelt toasts raised in honor of not just a boy who had dared to dream big and fought fiercely for something greater than himself, but also to acknowledge the hope and unity he had ignited among them. Leo, awash in gratitude and overwhelmed by the warmth of their affection, realized more profoundly than ever that he had indeed found a place within this village—a sanctuary where he belonged. He was no longer seen merely as a savior but as a crucial thread woven into the fabric of their lives, where he had earned not just their admiration but their hearts and unwavering trust as well.

And in that pivotal moment, as the stars twinkled overhead and the cool night air wrapped around him like a gentle caress, a revelation washed over him—the true, transformative power of gratitude. It was a force so potent that it could transform an entire community, acting as a unifying bond that could connect souls across the vast and unpredictable oceans of life. Gratitude went beyond merely acknowledging sacrifices—it was a warm light that fostered resilience, igniting hope and sparking a flame of inspiration that could illuminate even the darkest of paths. He understood now that in embracing this power, he not only celebrated his journey but also became a beacon of strength for others, reminding them of the limitless possibilities that arise when hearts open to one another.

Little did Leo know, this journey of gratitude was only the beginning of an extraordinary chapter in his life. In the gentle glow of this newfound appreciation, the seeds of purpose and determination took root deep within him, sprouting thoughts and aspirations he had never fully acknowledged before. As he reveled in the joyous smiles and infectious laughter that surrounded him, he could sense the powerful currents of change stirring in the depths of his being, like an undercurrent in a vast ocean—ready to carry him to uncharted territories filled with limitless possibilities.

With each passing moment spent with those who uplifted and inspired him, Leo began to understand that the bonds he was forging were not merely casual connections; rather, they were profound ties that would serve as guiding lights in the journey that lay ahead. These relationships, woven together with threads of shared experiences and mutual support, would lead him toward new adventures brimming with excitement, new challenges that would test his resilience, and perhaps even new roles that awaited him in the intricate tapestry of life that he was slowly beginning to comprehend.

As he stood amidst his newfound family, he felt an unwavering resolve bubbling within him—an inner strength that urged him to reach beyond the boundaries he had once accepted. He became acutely aware that he was no longer bound by the fears and insecurities that had once limited him. Instead, he was ready to fully embrace whatever came next with an open heart and a mind eager to learn. He felt a deep sense of empowerment, knowing that each step forward would not only shape his own destiny but also contribute to the collective journey of those around him. In that moment, surrounded by love and encouragement, Leo recognized that the adventure of gratitude had transformed into a powerful catalyst for growth, and with wide-eyed wonder, he prepared to venture into the exhilarating unknown.

Chapter 8

The sun hung low on the horizon, casting a warm and ethereal golden hue over the deep blue expanse of the ocean, reminiscent of molten gold poured delicately across a canvas. The day was stretching its legs, gently bidding farewell to the warmth of sunlight, and in its place, it promised the emergence of a starry spectacle. The sky transitioned gradually, shifting from bright, striking blues to soft pastels of lavender and blush, the colors weaving together in a breathtaking farewell to the day. As Leo stood on the weathered deck of his small boat, affectionately named the Ocean's Whisper, he marvelled at the sprawling vastness before him. It was a magnificent sight; each ripple and undulation of the water seemed to dance in sync with the pulse of the earth, creating a breathtaking symphony of sight and sound that enveloped him in its embrace.

With each wave that rolled beneath him, he felt a profound connection to the natural world, a sense of rhythm, as if the ocean was beating like a living heart, inviting him to join its eternal dance. It was as though the very essence of life coursed through the salty air and into his lungs, filling him with a sense of purpose. The serenity of the moment enveloped him, imbuing his spirit with tranquillity, yet an undeniable thrill surged through him, electrifying his senses. He was a sailor at heart, a wanderer yearning for adventure, and the sea represented the ultimate freedom, an open invitation to explore the mysteries that lay beyond the horizon.

Inspired by the captivating tales of exploration he had devoured in countless books and the vivid dreams that had haunted his nights, Leo decided it was time to step beyond the shores of familiarity that had cradled him for so long. It felt as if the ocean was calling to him, each wave a whisper enticing him to uncover the wonders hidden beneath its surface. He had conquered his fears, casting aside the limitations that had once tethered him, and fully embraced his unquenchable passion for water; now, it was time to dive headfirst into the uncharted waters that lay ahead. The tantalizing mysteries of the ocean whispered to him through the sound of crashing waves, and he could no longer resist their call; he was ready to discover what lay beyond the confines of his previous life.

As he set sail, the boat's sails billowed with the gentle but persistent sea breeze, propelling him towards distant horizons that stretched endlessly before him. Each gust of wind was an affirmation of his decision, a reminder that he was alive and carving his own path through the world. Leo carried with him more than just supplies; he brought his insatiable curiosity, an eager spirit ready to uncover the secrets hidden beneath the vast undulating waves. The gentle breeze filled his sails, urging his small vessel forward, and imagining what lay beyond each cresting wave sparked a fire within him—a vibrant world teeming with life, coral reefs bursting with colours vivid enough to steal one's breath, shimmering shoals of fish gliding effortlessly through the water, and islands adorned with stories of ancient mariners and forgotten tribes woven into their sandy shores.

Days turned into weeks as Leo sailed across the undulating surface of the sea, embraced by the elements that flanked him on his journey. The sun rose and set with an astonishing beauty, each sunrise painting the sky anew, while sunsets spilled hues of amber and crimson into the horizon's embrace. Each moment was an awe-inspiring gift, the ocean revealing a symphony of sights and sounds, each spectacle more wondrous than the last. Dolphins leapt alongside his boat, their playful antics illuminating his heart with uncontained joy and reminding him that he was undeniably alive in this vast, wild space. Their sleek bodies glistened in the fading light, and their cheerful clicks and whistles harmonized with the gentle lapping of the waves. At night, the sky transformed into an endless tapestry, as stars stretched across the velvet canvas above like diamonds scattered by a celestial hand. They twinkled cheerfully, guiding his path and urging him to dream bigger, to chase the horizon with the fervour of his imagination—a reminder that the universe was vast, filled with infinite possibilities.

However, the journey was not without its trials. One fateful night, a tempest roared to life, sweeping through the waters with fierce determination. The wind howled like a wild animal, lashing against the sails, and the waves loomed above his boat like treacherous mountains, fierce and unyielding. Rain hammered down, drenching him to the bone, while the thunder rumbled, adding a dangerous rhythm to the chaos around him. But Leo was resolute; he fought valiantly against the storm, his hands gripping the helm as his heart raced with adrenaline, fueled by a mix of fear and exhilaration. In that chaotic moment, as the gale raged around him, he understood the ocean's fierce beauty—the paradox of tranquillity and turmoil it embodied, the delicate balance it maintained.

With every ounce of strength and will, he navigated through the storm's fury, trusting in his instincts and the resilience he had cultivated during his time at sea. As he battled against the elements, he found clarity and strength within himself that he had not known existed. Finally, as dawn broke, a radiant light spilled across the water, illuminating his path and bathing him in a rebirth of hope. The storm receded, its violent whispers replaced by the soothing sounds of gentle waves. He emerged on the other side, breathless but alive, with a deeper respect for the sea's power etched into his soul—a reminder that every adventure comes with its challenges, but it is in overcoming them that true growth occurs. With his spirits buoyed by the victory over nature's wrath, Leo stared into the horizon, eyes alight with the promise of more adventures that awaited him in the deep blue beyond.

After the storm had finally passed, Leo found himself washed ashore on a remote island, one that had not yet captured the attention of cartographers and remained unmarked on his navigational charts. Curiosity surged within him like the tides of the sea, invigorating his spirit as he anchored his boat safely, the waves lapping gently against its hull. Stepping onto the pristine sand, he felt the delicate grains shifting beneath his feet, each one a testament to the artistry of nature, sculpted beautifully by the relentless kiss of the ocean.

The island appeared untouched by time, a secluded paradise preserved in a state of idyllic beauty that seemed to hold its breath, waiting for an explorer like him to unveil its mysteries. The air was alive with an electric tension, impregnated with the promise of discovery—a tantalizing whisper that beckoned him toward adventures yet to come. As he ventured further, the lush greenery welcomed him into its embrace, where vibrant blossoms swayed gently in the breeze, their colors almost luminous under the relentless gaze of the midday sun. The enchanting song of exotic birds filled his ears, creating a symphony that harmonized with the gentle rustle of whispering leaves, all alive with the essence of the island.

As Leo meandered deeper into this uncharted territory, he stumbled upon a site that piqued his interests—a collection of ancient stones, their weathered surfaces adorned with intricate carvings and hieroglyphs that spoke of a civilization long forgotten to the relentless march of time. Each carefully etched stroke was a testament to stories of explorers and adventurers who had once traversed these waters, driven by an insatiable thirst for knowledge and a desire to connect with the world. In that moment, an enlightening realization washed over Leo; he was not merely an observer of these relics; he was a vital continuation of a noble lineage of adventurers, bound to those audacious souls who had dared to look beyond the horizon and heroically embrace the life of exploration.

Inspired by the remarkable artefacts of the past, Leo chose to linger on the island, spending countless days meticulously documenting his findings—the diverse flora, the vibrant fauna, and the myriad hidden secrets that the island held tight within its verdant heart. With each discovery, he felt the weight of history's passage pressing upon him, urging him to perceive not only the ocean's surface but also the multifaceted depths of history that lay concealed beneath. He gathered seashells, each one uniquely formed and patterned, as if they were relics of stories waiting to be uncovered. With every new find, whether it was a peculiar shell, an ancient carving, or a fleeting moment captured in the graceful dance of a bird soaring through the canopy, he felt an increasingly profound connection to the larger mysteries of the world, as if the ocean's whispers had enveloped him, drawing him closer into its boundless embrace. It was clear that the journey had only just begun, and Leo was more than ready to follow where the currents of adventure would lead him next.

As Leo's time on the island slowly drew to a close, a bittersweet pang gripped his heart. He realized that this extraordinary journey had evolved beyond the mere act of exploration; it had become a profound voyage of self-discovery, peeling back the layers of his identity and revealing the true essence of who he was meant to be. The island, with its breathtaking landscapes and hidden treasures, had provided the perfect backdrop against which his internal transformation unfolded in a tapestry of experiences. He had faced terrifying storms that relentlessly tested his grit and resilience, embraced the breathtaking beauty of sunrises and sunsets that painted the sky in vivid hues, and listened to the whispers of the past that echoed through the rustling leaves and crashing waves.

With the sails unfurled and the wind filling the expansive canvas of his ship, Leo prepared to set out once more, carrying with him not just the practical knowledge gleaned from his adventures but also a deep-seated appreciation for the vastness and complexity of the ocean and all its myriad wonders. Each wave held a story to tell, each breeze whispered a lesson, and each moment spent in the embrace of the sea was a profound opportunity for personal growth and understanding.

As he gazed out toward the horizon that stretched endlessly before him, Leo felt an infectious smile bloom across his face, the kind that ignited a vigorous spark of excitement within his very core. He was prepared—ready to embrace whatever lay ahead and equipped with the understanding that the ocean's secrets were intricate and countless, each one beckoning him ever deeper into its enigmatic depths. At that moment, with the salty air filling his lungs, he recognized himself as a willing traveler, not merely a tourist wandering along a predetermined path but rather an intrepid explorer fully committed to a journey that would never truly end, a journey filled with anticipation, wonder, and an unquenchable thirst for discovery.

As he cast a final glance back at the island—now a mere speck in the distance against the expansive blue of the ocean—Leo came to a profound realization that echoed within the very core of his being. Every journey, he understood, reshapes the soul in myriad ways, peeling back layers to reveal hidden facets of courage, resilience, and an insatiable curiosity that had always lain dormant within him, patiently waiting for the right moment to emerge from the depths of his spirit. This voyage was more than just a physical departure; it was a metamorphosis of the self, a transformation that would unveil strengths he had never fully grasped he possessed.

The ocean, with its relentless waves and shimmering surface, was not merely a vast body of water; it symbolized so much more—a boundless realm of adventure that beckoned him to explore its mysteries. It served as a poignant reminder that the journey itself holds as much, if not greater, significance than the destination to which one aspires. The thrill of discovery, the unexpected moments of joy and challenge, these were what truly enriched his life and molded his character.

With this understanding firmly rooted in his heart and guiding his actions, Leo cast away from the familiar shores, leaving behind the safety of the known as he sailed into the vast unknown. The wind danced around him, its brisk embrace invigorating, while the waves surged beside him like a chorus of encouragement—cheering him on as he ventured forth into uncharted waters. Each gust of wind filled his sails with a sense of purpose, and his heart swelled with the intoxicating mix of wonder, anticipation, and dreams yet to be fulfilled.

He felt an exhilarating thrill at the prospect of the challenges and discoveries that lay ahead on this new leg of his journey. With every passing moment, he became increasingly aware that each new experience would continue to shape him in ways he could only begin to imagine, pushing the boundaries of his understanding and capacity.

At that moment, as the sun dipped lower in the sky and painted the horizon in hues of gold and crimson, Leo felt fiercely alive, as if he was suspended in a thrilling chapter of his unfolding story. His spirit, once perhaps restrained by the comforts of the familiar, now soared freely, ready to write the next pages of his life with courage, an insatiable thirst for knowledge, and an indomitable spirit. The world stretched endlessly ahead of him, full of promise and uncertainty, and he was determined to embrace it all with open arms, ready to discover who he was destined to become.

Chapter 9

Leo stood at the helm of his small but sturdy sailboat, the Ocean's Whisper, feeling the wind cradle him in its refreshing embrace. The sky overhead was a brilliant azure, painted with whimsical clouds that seemed to dance in time with the waves below, forming a picturesque canvas that captivated his spirit. This was freedom—an adventure he had always dreamed of embarking upon. Each day brought new discoveries, whispering secrets of the unfathomable depths, and today was destined to unfold extraordinary moments.

As he navigated deeper into the azure embrace of the ocean, Leo's eyes sparkled with fervent anticipation. The endless horizon stretched before him, an inviting guide into realms untouched by most, the promise of adventure hanging palpably in the salty air. He recalled a captivating tale told to him by an old sailor in a charming coastal town—a legend that spoke of an eccentric archipelago, a collection of islands where aquatic wonders roamed freely, where the very spirits of the sea played exuberant games, coaxing laughter from every wave. His heart raced at the thought of discovering these mythical islands, places that had danced through his dreams and illuminated his imagination for years.

Suddenly, as if summoned by his thoughts, Leo felt a gentle nudge against the side of his boat. He turned, his breath catching in his throat, to see a lively group of dolphins leaping joyfully through the surf, their sleek bodies glistening under the warm sun like polished silver. With a grin stretching across his face, he tossed a rope overboard, and to his delight, one particularly curious dolphin zipped closer, its big, inquisitive eyes sparkling with mischief and curiosity. This playful encounter served as a gentle reminder that the ocean was not just a vast expanse of water; it was a vibrant, living entity, teeming with magical creatures and endless possibilities.

"Come on!" Leo called out, his laughter melding beautifully with the exuberant shouts of the dolphins. One of them, a spirited creature he affectionately named Splash, raced alongside the bow, gliding effortlessly through the waves, their energy intertwining like a perfect symphony. Leo leaned over the edge, feeling the exhilarating spray of saltwater on his skin. When he dipped his hand into the cool sea, Splash surfaced beside him, playfully splashing him back, as if the creature were teasing a sibling in a delightful game. This moment felt like pure bliss; it was an unexplainable connection forged between man and nature, woven through laughter and joy.

Leo's heart raced with exhilaration. These enchanting creatures were not merely residents of the sea; they were companions in his grand adventure. He shared the horizon with them, each leap and dive an affirmation of life and freedom, swimming in the wild, exhilarating rhythm of the ocean. What began as playful antics turned into a joyous duet, as Splash performed spectacular acrobatics, twisting and turning with fluid grace through the water, while Leo erupted in delighted cheers, feeling the weight of the world melt away in the salty breeze. After a jubilant romp filled with laughter and splashes, the dolphins somersaulted away into the depths, leaving Leo with a rush of exuberant energy and a grin that stretched from ear to ear, infusing him with the invigorating essence of existence itself.

As the afternoon slipped into a luminous golden glow, Leo stumbled upon a vibrant cluster of coral reefs, bathed in the warm light of the sun cascading down like liquid gold. The colors were mesmerizing—a brilliant tapestry of deep oranges, electric blues, and radiant purples that pulsed with the very essence of life itself. It felt like stepping into a dream, a world where every hue painted a story of beauty and vitality. Without hesitation, he donned his snorkeling gear, and as he slipped into the crystalline waters, he was welcomed into an enchanting realm that enchanted his senses.

Under the surface, the world transformed. Schools of neon fish darted around him in a dizzying display of color and movement, their scales shimmering like tiny jewels beneath the sun's rays. Meanwhile, amorphous jellyfish floated gracefully in slow-motion, their translucent bodies trailing behind them like delicate lace, captivating him with their ethereal beauty as they glided through the water. Each breath he took was a reminder of the magic that existed just beneath the surface, pulsing with life and wonder, as Leo lost himself in the profound tranquility of the marine universe, each moment a cherished memory waiting to unfold in the grand tapestry of his adventure.

But the true magic unfolded when Leo stumbled upon a cove hidden beneath the majestic cliffs, its entrance cleverly concealed by towering rock formations that seemed to radiate a soft, ethereal light. As he cautiously approached, he felt a magnetic pull urging him forward. Inside the cove lay an enchanting underwater grotto, its entrance intricately framed by spiraling coral formations that resembled nature's own artwork—a stunning masterpiece sculpted by the patient hands of time, showcasing vibrant colors and intricate designs that danced in the gentle water currents.

With a heart full of wonder guiding him and a sense of adventure igniting his spirit, Leo took a deep breath and dove into the grotto. As he descended, he felt the water part around him like a curtain, welcoming him into this hidden world. The deeper he swam, the more his senses awakened, until he encountered something extraordinary: mermaids! These mythical beings, with their flowing hair cascading like glimmering waterfalls, glowed with an ethereal light. Their iridescent tails shimmered with every fluid movement, enchanting him entirely as they swirled around him, their laughter ringing like a melodious chorus that echoed against the grotto's walls, intertwining seamlessly with the gentle lapping of waves outside.

The mermaids beckoned him to join their whimsically enchanting dance, inviting him into a world of grace and beauty. They moved through the water with an effortless elegance, their movements fluid and hypnotic, as if choreographed to the rhythm of the ocean itself. Elated, Leo twirled and spun alongside them, surrendering to the joyous spirit that filled the watery realm. In those moments, he felt lighter than air, as if all of his concerns dissolved into the depths of the ocean. Ancient songs flowed around him, the melodies weaving a tapestry of connection to this magical existence he had only ever dreamt of, a reality that now embraced him warmly.

Time seemed to lose its meaning as the celebration ebbed and flowed, each moment stretching into eternity. His heart swelled with an overwhelming joy, and his spirit ignited by a profound sense of belonging, as if he had finally found a place where he was meant to be. The freedom he had long sought, that elusive feeling he had chased for so long, was not only waiting for him in the vast embrace of the ocean but was found in the welcoming arms of these enchanting beings who invited him wholeheartedly into their realm.

Amidst the playful splashes and effervescent laughter, as the mermaids danced with abandon, they suddenly noticed Leo's fascination with something glimmering on a nearby rock. He turned his gaze to find an exquisitely woven necklace of lustrous pearls, resting delicately on the smooth stone as if it were waiting just for him, a precious secret longing to be discovered. The pearls glimmered with an otherworldly light, each one whispering tales of the ocean's depths and its mesmerizing beauty—mysteries and stories waiting to be unveiled. With his curiosity piqued, Leo felt an irresistible pull toward this stunning piece of oceanic art, drawn in by the allure of the unknown, eager to uncover the secrets it held and further entwine his fate with the magical world around him.

One of the enchanting mermaids swam gracefully over to Leo, her long hair flowing like strands of silk in the water, and her eyes sparkling like the vibrant sea at dawn—a breathtaking sight radiant with hues of aquamarine that danced playfully, reflecting the first golden rays of sunlight peeking over the horizon. The sunlight pierced through the water's surface, casting a mystical glow that highlighted the shimmering scales of her tail, which glimmered in a mesmerizing array of blues and greens, reminiscent of the depths of the ocean itself. As she glided closer, Leo could feel the coolness of the water around him and the exhilarating rush of meeting such a mythical creature.

With a graceful motion, she extended her hand towards him, revealing a delicate shell, intricately carved with mesmerizing designs that seemed to tell tales of ancient oceanic lore. The shell's surface caught the light, illuminating details that depicted swirling currents and mysterious sea creatures—an exquisite token of friendship from the mysterious depths of the ocean. Her voice, melodious and soothing, floated through the water like a gentle siren's song, reminiscent of a soft breeze caressing his skin on a warm summer day, as she said, "For the sailor who dances with the waves." Leo felt a deep connection forming in that moment, as if the soul of the sea itself reached out to him.

With a heart full of gratitude and wonder, Leo accepted the precious gift, his fingers brushing against the smooth surface of the shell. He felt an overwhelming sense of connection to this enchanting world and the creature before him, knowing deep down that this moment would become a cherished memory he would carry with him throughout his entire life—a symbol of the extraordinary, enchanting world that lay beneath the waves, vibrant with life and full of mysteries waiting to be uncovered.

Reluctantly leaving the magical allure of the grotto behind, Leo turned his gaze to the vast, open ocean that stretched endlessly before him. He felt an exhilarating wave of excitement wash over him as he resumed his journey upon the blue expanse, his heart thrumming with the thrill of adventure. The sails of his vessel caught the brisk ocean winds, billowing outward like the wings of a mighty bird, propelling him forward as he charted a daring course through the labyrinth of waves. His destination was the remnants of forgotten ancient lore—sunken ships laden with secrets of the past and artefacts resting in silent repose beneath the shimmering surface, each whispering tales of those who had ventured before him.

Day by day, with a sense of wonder guiding him, Leo discovered sunken treasures that captivated his imagination—crates overflowing with shimmering gold coins that glinted in the light of the sun, and an array of jewels that sparkled like stars scattered across the expansive night sky. Each jewel seemed to hold the memory of its own journey, each one embedded with history and mystery. He meticulously documented every extraordinary find in a weathered, leather-bound notebook, where he sketched detailed maps and jotted down the captivating stories that would surely spellbind the inhabitants of the world above the water. To him, these treasures were not simply material wealth; they symbolized the untold stories of dreamers and adventurers who had traversed the treacherous seas long before him—kindred spirits who were united by the same wanderlust that coursed through his veins and inspired him to seek adventure beneath the waves. They were a reminder that he was part of a larger tapestry woven by courage, curiosity, and the endless pursuit of discovery.

As Leo emerged from yet another thrilling underwater exploration, he felt exhilaration coursing through his veins, invigorated by the wonders he had witnessed beneath the waves. Just as he breached the surface, an enchanting sight captured his attention—a colossal sea turtle gliding effortlessly through the mesmerizing azure waters. The creature seemed to float with an otherworldly grace, its ancient shell marked with the scars of time, each mark telling tales of resilience and survival in the vast ocean. Taking a deep, revitalizing breath, he instinctively dove back into the water to greet this gentle giant, his heart swelling with admiration at the sight of this serene being, a guardian of the ocean who carried the wisdom of ages in its tranquil, liquid gaze.

With a few powerful strokes, Leo reached the magnificent creature, climbing onto its broad, friendly back like a small child embarking on a whimsical adventure. The moment he settled in, an overwhelming sense of harmony enveloped him, an unspoken bond forged between human and turtle, as the magnificent beast navigated the great expanse of the ocean with an instinctive grace that resonated deeply within his very soul. Time seemed to stand still as they embarked on a playful journey together, exploring the mysteries of the underwater world.

The majestic sea turtle led Leo through secluded lagoons and to uncharted isles, its wise presence illuminating the paths lined with fragrant hibiscus blooms that swayed softly in the gentle breeze. The colorful petals danced as if greeting the duo, while the untouched beaches whispered secrets of serenity, inviting them to linger awhile longer. Together, they brushed through the thresholds of splendid places that were only whispered about in hushed reverence—hidden gems that defied the ordinary and ignited Leo's imagination. Each breathtaking landscape deepened his belief that the world was far more magical than he had ever dared to fathom.

In every new discovery, Leo felt an intrinsic connection to the ocean's ancient history, a tapestry woven with echoes of the past that intertwined effortlessly with his journey. As the ageless sea cradled his dreams and aspirations, it ignited an insatiable thirst for adventure within his soul—an urge to delve deeper into the heart of the ocean and unearth its endless mysteries.

As the sun dipped gracefully below the horizon, casting a warm, golden glow across the undulating waves, the sky underwent a breathtaking transformation. It morphed into a dazzling canvas, painted with hues of soft pinks and fiery oranges—a breathtaking masterpiece blending seamlessly into the deeper blues of the encroaching evening. Leo settled comfortably on the deck of his beloved sailboat, aptly named Ocean's Whisper, feeling the gentle rocking of the vessel as it tilted gracefully on the rhythmic waves. The cold, salty breeze played around him like a friendly spirit, ruffling his hair and sending a refreshing chill down his spine, a reminder of the vibrant world surrounding him.

He glanced down at the stunning necklace of lustrous pearls that lay against his chest, their iridescent sheen catching the last warm rays of sunlight and twinkling with an unspoken promise of the adventures yet to come. Each pearl seemed to pulsate with stories waiting to be told, and Leo cherished the magical bond they represented—a connection between the ocean's treasures and his own heart.

In that serene moment, as the world gracefully transitioned from day to night, Leo felt a profound sense of anticipation bubbling within his heart and soul. He understood in a way that transcended words that these magical experiences—each bursting with vibrant emotion and thrill—were merely the first chapters in a grand narrative waiting to unfold before him. The ocean had a way of inviting him to weave his tale, an exquisite blend of exhilaration and discovery, where every wave hinted at secrets yet to be unveiled and adventures yet to be embraced.

As twilight deepened, draping the landscape in a velvety cloak, Leo closed his eyes and inhaled deeply, savoring the mingled scents of saltwater and distant jasmine carried by the wind, each breath a reminder of the beauty surrounding him. With each inhalation, he envisioned future journeys that awaited him—an endless horizon filled with possibility. Where would the mysterious waves guide him next? His mind transformed into a vibrant canvas of imagination, and each adventure he had experienced rippled outward like concentric circles in a pond, pushing him further into the unknown. The thrill of exploration surged within him, a powerful current of inspiration urging him to dive deeper and seek out the wonders that lay concealed beneath the surface of a world teeming with life.

With a gentle, knowing smile playing upon his lips, Leo reopened his eyes to gaze at the star-speckled sky overhead. The stars twinkled like tiny jewels scattered across the deep indigo sea of night, ancient and timeless, all whispering secrets of explorers and adventurers who had come before him. They seemed to call out to him, urging him to chase after his dreams and let the currents of the ocean guide him to uncharted territories and hidden treasures. He could almost hear the distant call of adventure echoing in the rhythmic sounds of the waves as they lapped softly against the hull of Ocean's Whisper, a soft lullaby that thrilled his senses.

Indeed, the ocean was a living entity, alive and vibrant, teeming with stories just waiting for someone to listen and share them. In the depths of his being, Leo knew with unwavering certainty that this journey —this thrilling embrace of the unknown—had only just begun, and the most incredible tales were still waiting to be written. With a heart overflowing with hope and a spirit eager for adventure, he positioned himself at the helm of his beloved boat, ready to set sail into the enchanting mysteries of the night that beckoned just beyond the horizon. The open sea awaited, promising boundless opportunities for discovery, connection, and the unfolding of his one-of-a-kind story.

Chapter 10

The once serene sky, which had been a tranquil canvas of endless blue stretching infinitely above, had transformed dramatically into a raging battlefield of dark, swirling greys and blacks, each ominous hue swirling violently against its backdrop as if the heavens themselves were poised for war. It felt as if the universe had taken a deep breath, filling its lungs with fury, ready to unleash it upon the unsuspecting Earth below. Leo squinted fiercely, his eyes narrowed to slits, desperately attempting to shield his face against the relentless barrage of salty spray that clung to his skin like an unwelcome shroud, heavy and damp. His hands strained around the helm of his small sailing boat, aptly named Ocean's Whisper, as he fought valiantly to keep her steady amidst the chaos. Each tremor of the craft beneath him echoed the tumult of his inner turmoil, a poignant reminder that this journey was no longer a leisurely sail but an arduous battle between man and nature.

Above him, dark clouds rolled ominously, swirling in a sinister dance that seemed almost alive, casting deep, foreboding shadows across the ocean's surface. The water roiled and surged, reflecting the unpredictable moods of the sky, a stark reminder of nature's raw and unrestrained power. With each blink, Leo felt as though the storm was stealing his confidence, wrapping his determination in thick tendrils of dread that choked the air from his lungs. His heart pounded rapidly, a wild drumbeat echoing within his chest as the wind began to howl—a chilling clarion call announcing the approach of chaos—an unyielding specter lurking just beyond his control.

Leo had sailed countless voyages before, a series of adventures imbued with wonder and excitement as he glided across placid waters and felt a sense of freedom unlike any other. The gentle waves would often seem to share whispered secrets, stories of far-off places and uncharted territories waiting to be discovered. Yet on this day, everything felt undeniably different, as though an unseen storm had merged with the tempest raging in his mind—a palpable sense of impending doom loomed abundantly large on the horizon, chilling him to the bone. He peered into the tumultuous waters swirling beneath him, feeling Ocean's Whisper tilt precariously as if she too sensed the danger that fast approached, her wood creaking in protest against the fury of the elements.

"Stay calm, Leo," he muttered under his breath, his voice barely reaching the threshold of his ears amidst the clamor and chaos surrounding him. "You've faced worse." Just a week earlier, he had navigated through treacherous reefs, exuberantly swimming amongst playful dolphins—joyful creatures that danced and leaped through the aquamarine waters, embodying the very essence of freedom as they laughed and tumbled like carefree fish caught in the tide. Nature had always been both his cherished friend and fearsome foe, a duality he had learned to respect through many encounters, but never had it unveiled such a ferocious face as it did now, glaring down upon him with an intensity that sent shivers down his spine. He realized, with an awareness that felt almost overwhelming, that he was still just a novice sailor at best, and the sheer ferocity of the storm far exceeded anything he had ever previously learned in the comforting security of the marina.

As if on cue, the first wave slammed against the bow without warning, sending a sudden surge of cold ocean water cascading across the deck, drenching him from head to toe in icy despair. Gritting his teeth against the elements, Leo wrestled fiercely with the sails, desperately trying to secure them against the howling gale that threatened to tear them asunder, ripping apart his hard-fought plans as if they were mere strands of spider silk. The roar of the sea was deafening, a tumultuous symphony that echoed the frantic rhythm of his own racing heart, a chorus of chaos and cacophony that threatened to drown him in its relentless embrace. Panic climbed up his spine like a relentless serpent, ready to constrict him and squeeze out any remnants of rational thought; yet, he fought it down fiercely, summoning every ounce of determination from deep within his core, drawing upon reserves of strength he had scarcely known existed—the fire of survival igniting within him.

A fierce gust suddenly knocked Ocean's Whisper sideways, and Leo stumbled, grappling in vain at the rail to remain upright as the tempest raged around him. The relentless waves slammed against him with a vengeance, the tendrils of water seeking not only to overwhelm him but to seep into the innermost crevices of his mind, drowning his thoughts in a deluge of fear and uncertainty. Flashes of safer harbors filled his thoughts, vivid memories of sunlit beaches and warmth swirling in his mind like comforting silhouettes. But now, in the belly of the storm, they felt like mere illusions—taunting mirages within a nightmare he couldn't shake off. The balance between hope and despair swayed ominously, and Leo felt the weight of the world pressing down upon him, doubting whether he could escape the clutches of this storm alive. His heart thundered more loudly than the waves crashing against his small vessel, a resonant echo of the battle he fought, the quest to be more than just a sailor adrift on a turbulent sea.

"Focus!" Leo shouted, his voice nearly being consumed by the howling wind, a fierce reminder that the elements were not to be trifled with. He found himself grappling with the teachings imparted by his mentor, the legendary Old Captain Vance, whose rugged voice echoed in Leo's mind—each lesson a lifeline in this swirling chaos. These were the moments that tested a sailor's mettle, where survival hinged on the ability to recall not only the basics but also the finer points of seamanship that were ingrained in him through years of diligent training. Secure the sails and maintain the steering—these fundamental tenets of navigation flashed through his mind like neon signs, bright and vivid against the backdrop of the roaring tempest. Stay afloat. Above all, keep the boat pointed directly into the waves to navigate safely through the turbulent maelstrom that threatened to engulf him.

With a newfound sense of purpose igniting within him like a beacon in the storm, Leo pulled himself resolutely back to the helm, leaning into the storm as if to embrace the chaos that ebbed and flowed with an untamed fury around him. He anchored his resolve deeply, acutely aware that not just his life, but the lives of others hung in the balance; each decision he made could spell the difference between survival and disaster. The storm was a furious beast, rearing its head with a vengeance, its power palpable in the air; but he had already journeyed through countless tempests, each trial fortifying his spirit, too brave and too skilled to be shackled by fear now.

As the rain began to fall in heavy sheets, cold torrents hit him like icy daggers, biting into his skin relentlessly. The miserable downpour, a cascade of nature's anger, only fueled his determination to ride out the tempest—he would not succumb. Suddenly, from the swirling chaos, a colossal wave materialized ahead of him, a monstrous wall of water rising ominously from the horizon. It loomed larger than any he had ever encountered in his life, an unyielding titan that cast a shadow, a pall over him that felt almost smothering. Time seemed to contort around him, stretching into an agonizing slow motion, each quickened heartbeat echoing loud and frantic, sounding a rhythm that battled the thunderous roar of the tempest waging war all around him.

"Here we go!" he yelled defiantly, his voice nearly drowned out by the cacophony of the storm's wrath. With a steady grip on the helm, he steered Ocean's Whisper bravely into the oncoming swell, the boat's bow slicing through the face of the great wave as they embarked on this treacherous dance with destiny. For a heart-stopping moment, suspended in time, it felt as though they had transcended the physical realm, achieving a surreal weightlessness, balanced atop the world itself. But the fleeting pause was abruptly shattered as, in the next heartbeat, the boat plunged violently into the churning abyss below, swallowed whole by nature's unforgiving fury, as the wave broke over them with a roar that shook the very core of Leo's being.

Water surged relentlessly over the deck once more, a foamy torrent that threatened to engulf everything in its path. Leo struggled fiercely, muscles straining against the chaotic roiling of the sea, clawing with every ounce of strength to keep his head above the tumultuous waters. The storm was a living creature, fierce and untamed, hurling waves against the hull as if it were dispensing the fury of a vengeful god. Each crash reverberated through the wood, echoing a deep, primal challenge that resonated in Leo's chest, a battle cry reaching deep into his soul.

Yet, amid the cacophony of chaos, a flicker of calm ignited within him, a remembrance of his rigorous training: the countless hours spent honing his skills, navigating through ferocious conditions, learning to harness the tempest's energy, to embrace its wildness instead of resisting it. He had been taught that within chaos lay opportunity, a chance to rise above fear and seize control. And now, in this moment of truth, it was time to put that knowledge to the ultimate test.

"Steady!" he barked at himself, a fierce mantra against the relentless assault of the raging sea. He dug his feet firmly into the deck, grounding himself, feeling the boat rise and fall beneath him, a living entity that responded to the calls of the waves with an instinctual grace that inspired trust. Leo steadied his breath, forcing himself to become one with the rhythm of the storm, allowing its unpredictable power to flow through him instead of against him. This was a dance of survival, a test of wills between man and nature.

Just as he felt himself settling into a delicate balance, the wind shifted with a cruel twist, howling with newfound ferocity, whipping through the rigging and slapping the rain against his face like a thousand stinging needles. Thunder rolled overhead, a deep, resonant growl from a giant beast lurking in the sky, and suddenly, the heavens split apart with a blinding flash of lightning. For a heart-stopping instant, the world was illuminated, revealing the chaotic tableau surrounding him in stark and terrifying clarity. Every instinct in Leo's body screamed at him to abandon ship, to seek solace and safety back on dry land. But abandoning ship was not in his nature; he bore the heart of a fighter, infused with a fierce determination to battle the storm with every fiber of his being, resolute in his commitment to navigate through the chaos and emerge victorious. With the ferocity of the wind and sea urging him on, Leo prepared to face down the very elements themselves, embodying the spirit of a true sailor against all odds.

With a final, steely resolve, Leo adjusted the sails that flapped wildly in the ferocious wind, guiding them with expert precision to catch the gusts that still dared to dance around him with a defiant fury. The boat thrashed beneath him, yet he felt every sinew and muscle in its frame engage as it surged forward, propelling itself through the relentless grasp of the storm that raged like a wild beast. It was a fierce partnership forming before his eyes—an alliance forged in the heat of struggle, where the boat and sailor became entwined in a symbiotic bond, battling against the uncontrollable forces of nature.

Seconds stretched into what felt like hours, each fleeting moment a raw confrontation with the wild, untamed power of the storm. The sky roared, and the sea heaved, yet Leo remained steadfast, refusing to let go of the wheel. Just as unpredictably as it had begun, the tempest gradually began to subside, releasing its stranglehold on him. The furious winds, which had once screamed like anguished spirits, now softened into a gentle whisper; the torrential rain that had lashed against him transformed into a soothing drizzle, almost musical in its cadence. The monstrous waves, towering and chaotic moments before, began to settle into a rhythmic dance of surrender, yielding to the calm that followed the chaos—a calm welcomed with open arms.

Exhausted, waterlogged, and trembling with the last remnants of adrenaline coursing through his veins, Leo finally succumbed to the weariness that enveloped him like a heavy cloak. He dropped to his knees, a momentary retreat from the fierce battle he had fought and won against nature's fury. As he looked out toward the horizon, he saw the dark, threatening clouds parting like a curtain drawn back, revealing a brighter, serene world that lay just beyond. Rays of sunlight broke through the remnants of gloom, bathing the deck in a warm, golden glow that seemed to promise renewal and hope.

The tempest had tested him in ways he had never imagined possible, pushing him to confront not only the external storm that raged around him but also the tempest that brewed within his soul. Yet, against all odds, he emerged from its clutches—battered and bruised, yes, but unbroken. It was a true testament to the indomitable spirit of resilience that had lain dormant within him, now awakened and ignited anew like a flame fanned by a gust of wind. With a newfound strength, Leo stood tall, eyes fixed intently on the horizon, knowing that he had faced one of nature's fiercest challenges and had triumphed. He was ready to embrace whatever lay ahead, with courage and determination coursing through his veins.

As the last remnants of the storm faded into the distance, Leo took a deep, shuddering breath, allowing a profound sense of gratitude to envelop his being like a warm embrace. In that fleeting moment, he pondered the very essence of the storm that had raged around him. Perhaps it was not merely a tempest of nature that he had witnessed; perhaps it represented a rite of passage, an essential upheaval in his own life. One that was designed to prepare him for the myriad challenges that awaited him in uncharted waters. The power of the sea was undeniably magnificent, and Leo felt its wisdom coursing through his body, as if the ocean itself was imparting invaluable lessons with every crashing wave, teaching him that strength and resilience were often born from turbulence.

As his gaze remained fixed on the horizon, his heart swelled with anticipation for the next adventure that awaited him beyond the calm. He recognized that even amidst the chaos and tumult of the storm, there always lay a promise—an unwavering glimmer of hope that whispered sweetly in his ear: a brighter day was on the verge of breaking. This conviction illuminated his spirit, offering a comforting sense of direction and purpose amidst the swirling uncertainty that life presented.

With that hopeful vision shimmering brightly within his heart, Leo squared his shoulders, and a definitive resolve settled into his frame like armor. He felt invigorated, inspired, and unafraid, ready to embrace whatever lay ahead. The challenges may be daunting, the winds may howl, and the waves may crash with ferocity, but Leo knew he possessed the fortitude to navigate through any storm that life could throw at him. Determined to face each obstacle with the same fierceness as the elements surrounding him, his spirit remained unbroken, his resolve unyielding. Though he understood the journey ahead may be arduous, Leo was ready to set sail once more—confident in his ability to rise above and discover the treasures that awaited him beyond the tempest, for his heart was now a vessel of hope, sailing toward an endless horizon of possibility.

Chapter 11

With a heart racing as if it were the very storm that had raged around him, Leo stood precariously at the cliff's edge, his feet planted firmly on the weathered rock, gazing out across the tumultuous sea that roared below. The waves crashed violently against the jagged cliffs, sending up plumes of salt and spray that mingled with the darkening sky, creating a chaotic symphony of nature's wildness. Lightning danced overhead, illuminating the swelling clouds with an ominous brilliance; each flash served as a stark reminder of the raw, unyielding power that surrounded him and the monumental challenge that lay just ahead.

For weeks, he had steeled himself for this moment, mentally and emotionally preparing for what would become a pivotal point in his life. Each day had been a new undertaking—he trained relentlessly, pouring over ancient texts and seeking counsel from those who had faced similar trials. He understood that the trial he faced now would not only define him as a wielder of elemental power—an elusive title whispered among those who had witnessed his abilities—but it would also forge his identity as a person, as a friend, and as a beacon of hope for those who depended on him. The weight of anticipation bore down on him, intertwining with the fierce winds that whipped around him, creating a symphony of pressure that echoed his own racing heartbeat. Below, he felt the collective breath of the villagers rising, a chant of faith and fear, wrapping around him like the tempestuous winds.

The villagers had gathered at the base of the cliff, their faces a mix of anxiety and awe, dimly illuminated under the pall of the storm that loomed ominously overhead. The atmosphere was thick with tension, their murmurs weaving through the gusty air like the very threads of fate itself. Each voice barely rose above the roars of the sea and wind, a fragile symphony of uncertainty and hope, as they speculated whether Leo would rise to the monumental challenge or succumb to the fury of nature that threatened to engulf him. The legend of the

Stormbearer—a warrior said to possess the unparalleled ability to bend the tempest to his will—washed over the crowd like an ethereal wave, connecting them through shared myths. Yet the villagers had learned over time that legends are sometimes born from desperation and faith, crafted not merely from the marked deeds of heroes but from the hearts of those who dared to believe in their existence. The tales they told were as much about their own hopes as they were about any singular hero.

Taking a deep breath, Leo grounded himself, feeling the chilled air fill his lungs, igniting a fire deep within his core that surged to life with renewed vigor. The air around him was thick, charged with both energy and expectation—an almost palpable force crackled through the atmosphere, making the hair on the back of his neck stand on end. He focused his mind, visualizing each wave and gust as living beings—surging, howling, and pulsating with chaotic energy. The tempest seemed to rise and fall in an intricate dance, and he felt the tendrils of their fury pressing against him, testing his resolve, measuring his mettle against their unyielding power. It was a primal force, one that could consume him whole if he faltered even for a moment, yet he was determined to channel it, to become one with the storm instead of shying away from its full might.

But Leo did not falter. Drawing upon the depths of his being, he reached within himself to reconnect with the warmth of the fire he had nurtured all his life—a fire that had grown stronger and more vibrant with every trial and tribulation, every moment of doubt he had faced. It ignited within him, bright and fierce, merging seamlessly with the essence of the storm that raged around him. He could feel its rhythm, a resonating pulse that echoed through the wind and the water, syncing with his own heartbeat—a powerful reminder that he was indeed part of this ferocious dance. Each pulse brought with it the weight of destiny, as Leo took a step closer to the precipice, ready to face whatever lay ahead and to prove not only to the villagers but to himself that he was the embodiment of the legend they so ardently believed in. Would he command the storm's fury or would he be engulfed by it? He resolved to find out.

"Cease!" he commanded, his voice rising above the howling wind, a powerful decree that pierced through the chaotic symphony of nature's wrath. His voice reverberated with an intensity he had never known he possessed, a deep and resonant sound that traveled through the air like a strike of lightning. For a heartbeat, the world seemed to pause, suspended in a delicate moment of breathtaking suspense, captured in a fragile equilibrium teetering between chaos and calm. The storm did not relent immediately; it roared defiantly, a tempest unleashed. The wild winds clutched fiercely at him, twisting and curling like an enraged serpent, as if to mock his audacity and daring. Yet, in that very moment of defiance, a spark ignited within him—a flicker of resolve that transformed into a blazing fire. He visualized the storm as a fierce beast, untamed and relentless, one he was determined to tame—a task laden with treacherous risks and great uncertainty.

"Calm!" he shouted, his arms outstretched toward the ominous sky that pulsed with a light both eerie and electric. The words burst forth from deep within him—an ancient incantation learned from the venerable master, imbued with clarity of purpose and an unyielding sense of authority. They flowed from his lips like a river, unrestrained and powerful. And, like a spell woven with profound intention, the storm began to respond to his call. Little by little, the wild winds—once ferocious and howling—began to calm, their banshee wails softening into a mere whisper that caressed the air gently, as if apologizing for their earlier ferocity. The monstrous waves that had threatened to swallow him whole began to settle, transforming from a churning nightmare into something far less intimidating, a restless but calming mass.

A hush fell over the crowd gathered below, as if the very essence of time had paused, their breaths mingling into a single, collective intake of wonder and disbelief. They stood entranced, witnessing what they had believed to be impossible, the manifestation of magic interwoven with sheer will. The momentary rapture of Leo's voice permeated the very fabric of nature itself; he had transformed into one with the storm—an elegant steward bridging the mortal realm and the primal domain of the elements. The tumultuous hand of chaos, once so formidable and fearsome, began to fade gently into the peaceful embrace of serenity, like a receding tide relinquishing its hold.

As the clouds parted, unveiling a glorious sun, brilliant rays poured over the landscape, casting a warm, golden glow that illuminated the world anew. The village transformed under this celestial light, blossoming into a realm of boundless possibilities. The sea, once a churning beast that threatened to consume all, now sparkled like a resplendent sapphire beneath the sun's gentle embrace, its surface shimmering with tranquillity, a mirror reflecting the serenity restored. Tremors of power coursed through Leo, an exhilarating rush that filled him with both awe and trepidation, invigorating yet simultaneously draining. His breath came heavy, laden with the weight of what he had just accomplished, as he lowered his arms. A wave of exhaustion cascaded over him, reminding him that even in the profound victory he had just achieved, there lay an inherent cost to wielding such immense power.

With the storm now tamed and quelled, Leo stood at the precipice of his fate, forever altered as he embraced the realities of the responsibilities that had only just begun to unfurl before him. Had he truly done it? The question echoed in his mind, reverberating through the corners of his consciousness as he stood atop the rugged precipice, a mixture of disbelief and awe mixing and swirling within him. With limbs trembling from both the adrenaline and the weight of his realization, he hesitated momentarily, stepping back from the cliff's edge, overwhelmed by the monumental achievement that had just transpired. Below him, the villagers erupted into exuberant cheers, their voices soaring into the air like vibrant musical notes that danced upon the gentle breeze—a joyful, newfound melody of hope that resonated deeply within the hearts of all who had borne witness to his extraordinary act. Their cheers blended into a chorus that echoed across the landscape, a celebration of life and renewal, each voice a testament to the courage and strength that had been awakened within them all. In that moment, Leo felt not only a hero but also a beacon of hope, touched by the divine forces of the world, intertwined with both the storm and the serene light that followed.

But amidst the overwhelming elation that surged through him, a profound sense of vulnerability washed over Leo, enveloping him like a chilly wave that rolled in from the sea, unbidden and intense. In the midst of celebration, he had gazed deeply into the abyss—a vast, teeming chasm filled with turbulent emotions, raw energy, and unbridled power ready to erupt at any moment. He had commanded forces of nature that dwarfed anything anyone else had ever achieved, yet in this singular moment of realization, he understood that wielding such incredible power was not merely an act of reckless abandon or bravado. No, it was about something far more significant, a deeper truth that weighed heavily upon his heart: the immense weight of responsibility that came hand-in-hand with such capabilities.

As he stood amidst the gathered crowd, breathing in the lingering remnants of the storm still swirling within him, Leo became acutely aware of those elusive threads that connected him to the world—threads woven from shared emotions, aspirations, and fears. This connection filled him with a sense of exhilaration, but it also instilled a quiet fear. Power could be a double-edged sword, and with it came the potential for both creation and destruction.

As the sun began its descent, casting long, dramatic shadows across the sprawling landscape and igniting the horizon with hues of orange and purple, Leo tilted his gaze skyward. It was in this moment of reflection and introspection that he grasped the profound truth he had been blind to amid his resounding triumph. Even at the pinnacle of his strength, he realized that a delicate balance must always be maintained. The clouds that had once cast a shadow over the sky might have vanished in the wake of his victory, but he understood with renewed clarity that storms were never truly gone; they are cyclical, an inseparable part of the world's natural rhythm. Life, with all its complexities and contradictions, encompassed both light and darkness, joy and sorrow—each necessary to appreciate the other fully.

Feeling his heart pounding fiercely in his chest, the rhythm matching the energy of the village surrounding him, Leo turned back to face the villagers, his family—who stood before him, their faces aglow with pride and admiration, their eyes shimmering with wonder. He had not only passed the ultimate test; he had faced not just a demonstration of his remarkable powers but a deeper examination of his very character and integrity. In that electrifying moment, he realized that he had emerged not merely as a master of storms but as a protector and guardian of those who relied on him, and that thought filled him with a fierce resolve.

Each cheer that resonated from the crowd echoed within him, reverberating like the steady thump of a drum, each beat a reminder of the bond they shared. It was more than just admiration; it was a connection rooted in trust and shared destiny. With a silent vow, he pledged to honor and cherish the extraordinary gift he had been granted—a gift that, while magnificent, came with its fair share of trials and tribulations.

And with that promise came an awakening—a new storm began to brew deep within his soul, ignited by a fierce resolve to safeguard the bond he now cherished with the world around him. This bond required him to navigate the ever-turbulent paths that lay ahead, armed with both heart and unwavering courage. Leo was no longer just a boy caught in the tempest of learning to harness the storm; he had transformed into the storm's guardian—a beacon of light amid the encroaching darkness, steadfast and resolute, poised to confront whatever challenges lay in wait.

In this nascent understanding, he comprehended that this test was merely the beginning of a much larger journey. The road ahead would undoubtedly be fraught with uncertainty, shadows lurking at every turn, but now, fortified with wisdom, a deep sense of purpose, and an indomitable spirit, he felt more prepared than ever. Leo was ready to embark on this transformative journey, committed to protecting his village and nurturing the fragile balance of nature that he had come to respect and revere deeply. The world was vast and unpredictable, filled with both challenges and opportunities, but with newfound determination, he was resolved to face it all, one storm at a time, guided by the knowledge that every obstacle was merely an opportunity to grow stronger in his resolve and understanding of the forces at play in both nature and within himself.

Chapter 12

As Leo continued his journey across the boundless, azure expanse of the ocean, he began to fully grasp the remarkable magnitude of his extraordinary powers, powers he had instinctively sensed but had never fully understood. Each wave that crashed against the sturdy hull of his boat seemed to resonate with a unique melody, a song bursting with complex emotions—an intricate symphony expertly composed of joy, sorrow, anger, and love, all interwoven like delicate strands of silk. The ocean, in all its vastness, was no longer merely a seemingly interminable stretch of blue; it had transformed into a living, breathing entity. Every single drop of saltwater was infused with the rich essence of its enduring history, its countless narratives and secrets waiting to be uncovered. Leo had always felt an invisible thread connecting him to the sea, a magnetic pull that drew him deeper into its enigmatic depths, but now, as he stood poised in the embrace of the water, he comprehended its profundity and significance in ways he had never imagined possible.

Standing resolutely at the bow of his vessel, he allowed the wind to playfully tease his tousled hair, the invigorating smell of brine filling his lungs and reminding him of life's boundless possibilities as he embraced the sheer exhilaration of the moment. He closed his eyes, surrendering himself to the tides of emotions that surrounded him, an enveloping warmth akin to a beloved embrace. The ocean began to whisper its ancient secrets into his mind: tales of valiant vessels lost to the inexorable depths, of courageous mariners who had defied the relentless grip of fate, and of monstrous storms that had once raged with apocalyptic fury only to yield to the serene calmness that dawn's gentle light promised. These stories wrapped around him like tendrils of mist, urging him to listen closely, to understand the language of the sea.

With each swell and dip of his boat navigating through the watery landscape, Leo felt the vibrant joy of dolphins frolicking nearby. Their playful leaps and acrobatics became a jubilant celebration of life itself, as if the very essence of joy had taken flight among them. Their spirits, light-hearted and uninhibited, filled him with an infectious laughter that bubbled up from within, echoing against the backdrop of the vast ocean. However, beneath that effervescent surface joy, he could sense deeper and darker currents swirling—those of sorrow that resonated in the soulful songs of whales, creatures that mourned their lost kin. Their mournful melodies reverberated over vast distances, pleading for healing and heartfelt understanding from the world above, an echo of loss that tugged at his very soul.

In that moment of profound introspection, Leo shifted his perception of himself. He had always thought of himself as merely a voyager, a seeker of adventure traversing the magnificent waters of the unknown. But now, clarity washed over him like a lighthouse's comforting glow guiding ships to safety. He realized that he was not only a master of the seas; he had evolved into something greater—a guardian and a fierce protector of their fragile beauty. This dawning understanding surged through him like an unstoppable tide, powerful and undeniable, filling him with a weighty realization—a responsibility that pressed heavily against his chest, urging him to act, to forge a deeper connection with the waters that nurtured the diverse tapestry of life but were also under threat.

"Leo!" a voice called out, shattering the spell of his reverie. It was Mira, his loyal and steadfast companion, who joined him at the bow, her warm brown eyes shining brightly with comprehension and curiosity. "You're glowing. What are you feeling?"

"The ocean," he breathed, the words spilling forth from him like an intimate confession, "it's alive, Mira. It's not just a body of water... it's a rich tapestry of emotions and stories that yearns to be understood. I can feel everything—the joy it holds, the pain it bears... it needs us."

Mira raised an eyebrow, her expression a mix of intrigue and curiosity. "What do you mean it needs us? What can we do to help?"

Leo took a deep, steadying breath, grounding himself as he gathered his thoughts. "We have to protect it. As we journey to the islands, we're uncovering so much. The pollution is suffocating it, the loss of coral reefs is devastating marine life, and the general disregard for its depths is undermining the very essence of what the ocean truly is."

Mira nodded slowly, her gaze thoughtful as she absorbed the gravity of his words. "We've witnessed it ourselves, haven't we? The plastic waste washing ashore, the helpless wildlife forced to adapt to a world that no longer accommodates them... but how can we make a difference? We are just two people on a boat."

"They won't just be two anymore," he declared with growing determination, an unstoppable swell of conviction rising within him like the tide. "We will reach out to others who feel this urgent call to action, gather them together, and raise awareness of the ocean's plight. We can be advocates for those who cannot speak for themselves. Look—" he pointed decisively toward the horizon, where the sun was gently setting, casting warm golden hues across the surface of the water. "Even the sea deserves to be heard, cherished, and loved. We have to become its voice."

As the sun dipped lower, painting the sky with brilliant oranges and purples, Leo felt a powerful surge of purpose coursing through him. This journey had transformed from a simple adventure into a profound quest—one aimed at awakening a collective consciousness, fostering a deep reverence for the natural world, and ensuring that the myriad stories of the ocean, both joyful and sorrowful, would continue to echo and inspire through time. Together, they would embark on a new chapter—not only to explore the ocean's breathtaking beauty but to fiercely safeguard its sanctity for generations to come. The journey had just begun, and its significance was destined to ripple far beyond the horizon.

As the last rays of sun delicately dipped below the horizon, night cloaked the ocean in a deep, velvety darkness, and a profound sense of empowerment surged through Leo's veins. The gentle lapping of waves against the hull of the boat transcended mere sound; it emerged as a symphony of existence that resonated within him, a call to respect and preserve life. This revelation expanded the bounds of his understanding, intertwining him with the very essence of life and nature itself. At that moment, he realized that he was not just an outsider, a solitary observer marveling at the wonders of the natural world; rather, he was a vital part of it, an integral thread woven into the intricate tapestry that made up the oceanic expanse. A deep connection wrapped around him, a bond that transformed him into a bridge linking humanity to the infinite vastness of the seas stretching endlessly beyond the horizon, inviting him to forge a pathway of understanding and action that would resonate through the ages.

With that newfound conviction radiating from his core, Leo lifted his gaze to watch as the stars began to twinkle into existence, piercing the darkening canvas of the sky. Each tiny, bright point shimmered like a beacon of hope against the yawning abyss, a reminder that even in darkness, there is light. This celestial display was not just a random scattering of distant suns; it was a profound symbol of the journey he was about to undertake—a journey of discovery, struggle, and eventual triumph. He understood that the journey ahead would be nothing short of profound—an odyssey filled with challenges as formidable as the mightiest of waves crashing against the rocky shore. These waves represented obstacles that could threaten to pull him under, yet their very existence invigorated him; they reminded him that tenacity was often born from turbulence. Each swell and trough resonated with the rhythm of life's unpredictability, underscoring the truth that beauty and chaos often intertwine.

Yet amid this uncertainty, he held onto a steadfast belief: with each step he took, he would carry the whispered voices of the ocean within him. Their stories, their struggles, and their triumphs would become his own, and he would endeavor resolutely to ensure that the ocean's narrative was shared and celebrated. The whispers of the ocean were more than mere sounds; they were a symphony of experiences, a chorus of resilience calling him to contribute to its unending saga. He could almost hear their stories—a chorus of lost sailors and triumphant explorers, narratives woven together by the ebb and flow of tides.

In his mind, Leo envisioned his partner, Mira, by his side, their strong spirits united in purpose. Together, they would rally allies from all corners, forging connections with fellow guardians of the sea—those who, like them, cherished the ocean's beauty and felt a kinship with its depths. They would share their visions and collective memories, igniting a sense of community among those who understood the ocean's significance. This vision was not just about partners; it expanded to include families, communities, and cultures tied to the water's edge, all of whom found solace and strength in its embrace.

They would rise together, a formidable coalition against the myriad forces that sought to tarnish the ocean's splendor. Each member of this alliance would carry their own stories, struggles, and hopes, each tale strengthening their collective resolve. Leo understood that the ocean was so much more than an expanse of water lapping against the shore; it embodied love and pain, dreams and regrets, an ever-unfolding tapestry of life continuing to weave its complex story. The depths were a mosaic of existence, encompassing flora and fauna, ancient shipwrecks and vibrant coral reefs, all intertwined in an intricate balance that demanded respect and protection. This world beneath the waves awaited those daring enough to embrace its calling, to immerse themselves in its depths, to become part of its unfurling saga.

And so, with a heart brimming with purpose and a mind sharpened by clarity, Leo stood poised on the brink of his true destiny, ready to answer the call of the ocean. He was not merely a witness but a participant in the grand narrative, ready to step forth into the unfolding adventure that lay ahead. The stars glittered above him, each one a silent witness to his commitment, urging him onward into the great unknown that awaited beyond the waves. They served not just as markers in the sky but as guides illuminating his path—a reminder that he was part of something far greater than himself, a force of nature destined to contribute to the legacy of the ocean and ensure its voice would not be drowned out but would resonate throughout the ages.

Chapter 13

The moon hung high over the ocean, a luminescent beacon in the vast, deep blue canvas of the night sky. Its silvery glow bathed the water in a soft, ethereal light, casting shimmering trails that danced across the undulating waves. Each glimmer illuminated the dark waters beneath, transforming them into a mesmerizing pathway of liquid silver, a path that seemed to lead somewhere far and beyond, inviting and alluring in its mystery.

Standing at the very edge of the cliff, Leo felt the world around him resonate with his own inner turmoil. The salt-laden breeze played whimsically with his hair, tousling it in wild disarray, while the crisp night air was intermingled with the warmth of his swirling thoughts. It was a dichotomy that mirrored his heart—an inner tempest brewing within him, raging between the forces of resolve and desire. Each surge of feeling crashed against the others, creating a cacophony that echoed within his core, a whirlwind of longing intertwined with ambition that surged and receded like the tides below.

The relentless crash of the waves served as a backdrop to his chaotic emotions, the sound reverberating through the night air and harmonizing with the symphony of his internal struggle. It was a powerful reminder of the extraordinary abilities that now coursed through him, a primal force that pulsed beneath his skin, alive and demanding to be set free. They called to him with an irresistible allure, whispering promises of unimaginable wealth, unyielding control, and an unrivaled dominance over the vast, untamed waters that had once simply been his humble home.

For months, Leo had thrown himself into the depths of his newfound powers, dedicating himself tirelessly to mastering the ethereal forces of nature he had come to possess. He learned to manipulate the tides as though they were mere strands of silk in his adept hands, guiding their ebb and flow with a fluid grace. He could summon winds so fierce they could stir the very ocean itself with just a flick of his wrist. He had even discovered the art of communicating with the vibrant array of marine life that thrived in the sunlit depths below, enchanting creatures of the sea who shared their secrets with him. No longer was he just Leo, the simple fisherman weathering life's storms; he had transformed into an elemental force, a conjurer of storms capable of bending nature to his indomitable will. Yet, as he stood there, staring deep into the shimmering cerulean depths of the ocean, an unsettling voice within him questioned whether this newfound identity came with a price too steep to bear.

His mind wandered beyond the horizon, conjuring vivid images of glittering gold coins spilling forth from ornate chests, treasures accrued over lifetimes of toil and adventure. He envisioned the silken drapery of opulent merchants in far-off lands, those who had fashioned their great fortunes from the bounty of the sea, their lives steeped in luxury and ambition. His imagination flickered with the allure of precious gems that sparkled like distant stars when kissed by the moonlight, treasures just waiting to be reclaimed from the depths below. With just a snap of his fingers, Leo could summon forth a bountiful harvest of riches from the forgotten sunken galleons—grand ships lost to time's relentless march, now entombed beneath layers of shifting sands and the ever-churning ocean floor. Yet just as the tides ebbed and flowed in unison with the moon's powerful pull, so too did the currents of his conscience—an unyielding, silent tide, ever-present and demanding in its own right.

The haunting legends of ancient mariners came flooding back to him, tales of those formidable souls who had once possessed the unfathomable power to command sea and storm. Some had become revered figures, their names etched into the annals of history like constellations in the night sky, guiding the lost and weary. Yet others had succumbed to madness, the intoxicating nature of their gifts leading them down dark paths of greed and despair. The sea—both a nurturing mother and a ravenous beast—could reward or consume as she saw fit. Many had been lost to their unchecked desires, swallowed whole by the very depths they had once so masterfully commanded. The whispers of the ocean shared tales of those who had become mere shadows of their former selves, haunting remnants of their own insatiable desires and the heavy toll of their choices.

Suddenly, a voice broke through the fog of his reflection, pulling his thoughts back to the present. The salty breeze stirred long-settled memories, clinging to him like barnacles clinging to the sides of forgotten ships. Stepping gracefully from the shadows, it was Mira, the sea nymph who had become both his mentor and steadfast friend. Her luminous figure emerged like an apparition of light in the darkness, her hair flowing like the waves at dawn, glistening with an ethereal glow that seemed to embody the very essence of the moonlit ocean. Mira had always been a guiding light for Leo, urging caution and warning him against the seductive allure of power that could so easily lead one astray. Yet here she stood now, drawn to the precipice of the cliff like a moth to a flame, her presence a blend of intrigue and caution that danced in the air around them.

In her eyes, he saw the reflection of the ocean—the potential for great beauty tethered to the danger that lurked just beneath the surface. A silent understanding passed between them, a reminder of the delicate balance between ambition and humility, power and responsibility. Leo took a deep breath, the tangy scent of the sea filling his lungs, grounding him in the moment as he caught her gaze. The waves crashed behind him, relentless and rhythmic, as he contemplated the crossroads before him. In that moment, he knew he stood on the brink of a choice that could alter the course of his life forever—the question remained: would he heed the wisdom of the sea, or would he allow his desires to plunge him into the depths of darkness?

"Leo," she said softly, her voice a soothing balm—gentle like the lull of distant waves against the shoreline, grounding him amidst the tempest of his thoughts, "what troubles you?"

He took a deep breath, grappling with the burgeoning storm within him, the conflicting desires that weighed heavily on his heart. "I could take so much, Mira. The wealth of the world is hidden in the oceans, buried treasures just waiting for someone brave enough to claim them. I can bring it all to the surface, to transform both my fate and the fate of countless others."

"But at what cost?" she pressed gently, stepping closer to him. The sea foam curled at her feet, dancing in rhythm with the waves as she regarded him with unwavering concern. "Your heart is not wicked, dear Leo, but the promise of power is a siren's call that can corrupt even the noblest of souls. Do not let your ambition drown out the whisper of your conscience, the part of you that knows the difference between right and wrong."

"I know," he replied, a hint of frustration lacing his voice, almost simmering just below the surface. "But think of what I could do with that power! I could protect the oceans from those who seek to plunder them! I could restore balance to the ecosystems that have suffered so greatly, ensuring no one ever has to endure the pain that I did. This could be a gift—a chance to be a force for good!"

Mira's expression remained serene but resolute, a picture of unyielding wisdom. "And yet, with every decision to wield that power for selfish gain, you open the door to potential ruin. The sea has a memory that spans centuries—it remembers every betrayal, every act of greed. It may bestow blessings, but it exacts its price in blood and tears. The trust you speak of is not easily regained once broken. So think carefully, Leo."

Her eyes held an ancient depth, understanding the tempest within him better than he did himself, a reminder that his path was not simply about the pursuit of power, but the stewardship of the ocean he so dearly loved. The night whispered around them, the waves crashing below echoing the conflicts that swirled within his heart and the heavy burden of choice resting on his shoulders. In that moment, Leo stood at a crossroads, the promise of greatness tangible and tantalizing, yet laced with the shadows of consequence. He had to choose wisely—for the tides of fate would not bend easily for those who tread lightly upon the spirits of the depths.

He shut his eyes, feeling the weight of her words sink deep into his heart, as a stone dropped into still water, sending ripples of thought cascading through his mind. Each syllable resonated with an unspoken truth, filling him with a sense of purpose that had been dormant for far too long. The ocean had always kissed the shores with its rhythmic patterns, whispering secrets that only those who truly listened could comprehend. It spoke of beauty and chaos, of creation and destruction, a delicate balance that he had come to respect through his countless encounters with it.

Whenever he summoned the waves or danced with the wind, he felt the closeness of the ocean's spirit wrap around him like a warm embrace, a reminder of the sacred dance of life that thrived beneath the surface. He had forged a bond with the sea, one rooted in respect and reverence—an understanding that the depths were not just a source of treasures or riches, but a vibrant world teeming with life and mystery. Each fish darting through the coral, each swell of the tide carried whispers of generations past, tales woven into the very fabric of the sea.

Could he tarnish that connection for the allure of fleeting wealth, the tempting promises of gold and fame that could so easily lead him astray? The ocean had taught him gratitude, resilience, and the importance of nurturing life rather than depleting it. Those priceless lessons echoed in the chambers of his mind, urging him to remember the simplicity of authenticity and the profound joy found in being a custodian rather than a conqueror.

He felt a stirring deep within, a rejuvenation of the fire that had once burned brightly in his spirit before the shadows of ambition began to cloud it. Mira's unwavering gaze anchored him; her faith in his integrity rekindled his resolve. He envisioned the potential of his journey—dreams held aloft in the hands of hope and guided by moral compass. If he chose wisely, the ocean would not only remain a source of inspiration but would also thrive under his guardianship.

With reopening eyes, he clenched his fists, the salt of the sea mingling with his resolve. He recognized now that great power could just as easily become a curse if wielded without wisdom; it was not merely about the treasures he could gather, but the legacy he would leave behind. The waves rolled forward, carrying the whispers of the past and the hope of the future, urging him to embrace not just his ambition but the responsibilities that came with it.

In that moment, Leo knew he had a choice that went beyond the immediate allure of wealth. He would strive to balance the fierce strength of his ambitions with the quiet wisdom of the ocean. He would become not just a seeker of buried treasures, but a protector of the very essence of life that flourished within its depths. A guardian, not just of his dreams but of the dreams of all who would come after him, echoing out like a song carried on the winds of change.

As Leo opened his eyes, the world around him transformed in an instant, coming sharply into focus. Vibrant hues flooded his vision, painting the landscape with a richness that he had never truly appreciated before. The sky above shimmered with a brilliant azure, while the ocean below sparkled, reflecting sunlight like myriad diamonds dancing with the waves. Leo felt a surge of adrenaline course through him, as if he were witnessing the world reborn. His gaze burned with newfound clarity, a deep-seated determination igniting within him, akin to the first rays of dawn spilling over a serene horizon.

With firm conviction, he proclaimed, "I cannot betray the sea." His voice rang out, steady and resolute, reverberating against the rocky cliffs that stood as stoic guardians of the shore. "I may barter with its treasures, but not for my gain." As each word escaped his lips, he could almost feel the heavy cloak of doubt lifting from his shoulders, replaced instead by a lightness, a liberating sensation that enveloped him. This was the effect of making a choice aligned with his true self, a decision that resonated with the very fibers of his being. He instinctively stepped back from the precipice, feeling the relentless pull of avarice finally relinquish its tenacious grip on him. He stood tall against the tempest of temptation, a warrior grounded in purpose.

Mira, standing beside him, smiled softly, her eyes sparkling with approval. A glow illuminated her ethereal features, enhancing her already otherworldly presence. "Then you are wise, Leo," she replied, her voice melodic and soothing, wrapping around him like a comforting blanket woven from the gentle whispers of the sea. "Power without purpose leads only to chaos, a wild tempest that can consume even the strongest of souls." Every word she spoke painted vivid imagery in his mind, amplifying the weight of the responsibility they were now sharing. "Together, we will protect the seas and nurture the harmony that dwells within, ensuring that the delicate balance of life remains undisturbed. Let us be guardians, not conquerors."

Mira's message resonated deeply within Leo's heart, filling him with an unshakeable resolve. The mission that lay before them was not one driven by personal gain or conquest; it was a calling to stewardship, a sacred trust to care for the world's treasures. Side by side, they would be champions of the ocean's ephemeral beauty, dedicating themselves to safeguarding its wonders for generations yet unborn. In that electrifying moment of clarity, Leo realized that true wealth was not quantified by material possessions, but rather by the love and respect he offered to the vast, flourishing world that surrounded him.

Motivated now by a deep and unwavering sense of purpose that surged within him like the relentless tides, Leo extended his hand toward the vast, shimmering ocean, surrendering himself to its captivating embrace. He could feel the subtle vibrations of life beneath the surface, a rhythmic pulse echoing the intentions of his heart. In that ephemeral yet potent instance, he envisioned a future unshackled from the chains of greed and self-interest. Instead, it was one anchored in a profound commitment to stewardship and respect for the natural world.

This vision called for him not to command the mighty tides but to honor them, to cultivate a reciprocal relationship between humanity and nature—a harmonious coexistence that would yield benefits for both. The intoxicating scent of saltwater mingled with the cool night air enveloping him, rich with the promise of new adventures yet to come. Above, the stars glimmered like distant guardians, their celestial light casting a protective glow, as if the universe were silently urging him on.

Turning back to Mira, there was a sense of solemnity in the responsibility that now rested upon his shoulders—a burden that felt both heavy and uplifting, much like the soft light of dawn illuminating the dark canvas of night. The seductive temptation that had danced around him, whispering sweet promises of riches, was now a fading memory, eclipsed by the conscious choice he had made to embrace a path characterized by integrity and purpose.

Together, Leo and Mira began their journey as protectors, their unwavering dedication lighting their way through the uncertainties ahead. They were equipped to face a multitude of challenges that awaited them, driven by a shared understanding that true power did not lie merely in what one could extract from the world, but rather in the loving contributions one could offer in return. It was this profound revelation that forged their bond, igniting their mission with passion and intent.

As they moved forward into the enveloping embrace of the night, the ocean responded in kind, a gentle whisper cradling their ears. It began to share its myriad secrets, now safe in the hands of its truest friends—two souls destined to illuminate the fragile beauty of the world. They were united in purpose, steadfast in their pledge to ensure that the splendor and majesty of the ocean would endure, flourishing for generations to come. Each step they took was a testament to their commitment, weaving them deeper into the fabric of a harmony that would echo well beyond their time, reverberating through the ages with the purest of intentions.

Chapter 14

The coastal winds swept in powerfully, their crisp, salty gusts enveloping Leo in a familiar embrace that he had come to cherish. He stood resolutely on the precipice of a towering cliff, every fiber of his being attuned to the spectacular vista that lay before him—the vast, unfathomable expanse of the sea stretching infinitely across the horizon, an endless blue that melded seamlessly with the sky. The water glimmered brilliantly, reflecting the soft amber glow of the morning sun, its surface resembling a grand canvas adorned in shifting shades of blue and green. Each hue danced gracefully, a harmonious ballet choreographed by the rhythmic undulations of the waves, echoing the heartbeat of the earth itself. This breathtaking panorama captivated his heart and stirred his very soul, luring him into a serene reverie. However, beneath the enchanting beauty of this coastal paradise, Leo felt the crushing weight of a heaviness that anchored his heart—a burden born from the gravity of a decision he had been grappling with for far too long.

For weeks, the ocean had been the silent witness to Leo's internal struggle, engulfed in a tumultuous battle fueled by temptation and desire. The raw, untamed power that coursed through his veins was intoxicating, a divine gift bestowed upon him, one that he held the potential to wield in ways that could alter the very fabric of nature itself. With a mere thought, he could summon the formidable might of storms, calming their rage as easily as a gentle breeze disperses morning mist. Fish would flock in abundance at his call, their scales shimmering like scattered jewels under the sun, and he could stand as a sentinel against the relentless forces of destruction that threatened to ravage the shorelines he loved. The allure of becoming a hero, a savior of the sea itself, beckoned to him like the siren's call, sweet and irresistible. Yet, deep within his soul, Leo understood the intricacies and complexities of such formidable power. He pondered silently, at what cost would his benevolent actions come?

Visions of the ocean's vibrant ecosystems swirled through his mind like ephemeral shadows flitting across the surface of his thoughts. He imagined schools of fish, their bodies darting playfully amongst the intricate coral reefs, and majestic whales breaching the surface with an elegance that seemed to defy the very laws of gravity and water. Flocks of seabirds soared overhead, their cries a joyful hymn that echoed the promise of freedom above the turquoise depths. For Leo, the ocean was not merely a picturesque backdrop for human industry; it was a living, breathing entity—an intricate web of life teeming with mysteries, rich with ancient stories waiting to be uncovered. Each crest of a wave was a testament to the continuity of existence, a jubilant celebration of nature's artistry. With every whisper of power that beckoned him, Leo felt the silent yearning of the ocean pulsing through him, its sacredness resonating in the very core of his being.

He closed his eyes for a moment, inhaling deeply, allowing the crisp, briny sea air to fill his lungs, as if he were trying to absorb the very essence of the ocean into his spirit. For as long as memory served him, diving beneath the waves had been his sanctuary—a second home, a sacred place where he felt an unbreakable connection with something far greater than himself. Yet, that bond now carried with it a tremendous sense of responsibility, a profound weight pressing upon his chest like a tempest gathering strength on the horizon. The wisdom of his mentor, Elyra, bubbled up from the depths of his mind—a sagacious woman, she had guided him with grace through the intricate dance of balance, teaching him the delicate art of nurturing and stewardship of the natural world. "With power comes the weight of choice, Leo. Each decision will ripple through the world; make those ripples count," she had impressed upon him, her words reverberating like timeless echoes through the corridors of his thoughts.

As her teachings washed over him, Leo could almost hear the laughter of the waves, their playful ebbs and flows that were both joyous and tinged with a melancholic undertone. They were not his to command nor to bend to his will; they were his allies, companions in a grand tapestry of life, both strangers and kin bound by a shared existence. Leo resolved within himself that he would not transform into a tyrant, wielding absolute dominion over their tides, for he understood that true power lay in partnership and respect. And so he stood at the cliff's edge, with the wind tousling his hair and the ocean calling to him, contemplating the path that lay ahead, knowing that his choices carried the weight of the world and the profound wisdom of the waters.

Far below, the water churned energetically as the relentless waves crashed against the rugged cliffs, reverberating a continuous heartbeat—a pulsating reminder of the vibrant life teeming just beneath the surface. The sound echoed around him—an auditory tapestry of energy and vitality, as if the ocean itself was breathing in and out in concert with the world above. In this profound moment, he envisioned the incredible array of creatures that called these waters home. Images of playful dolphins leaping and surfing joyfully through the frothy crests of waves danced in his mind, their sleek bodies glistening in the sunlight. He imagined graceful rays gliding effortlessly through the azure depths, moving like living kites, their wings outstretched in serene elegance. The thought of colorful fish weaving through coral gardens and the myriad of hidden wonders thriving within the dark embrace of the ocean filled him with awe. All these magnificent beings existed in a delicate balance, each one guided by their instincts and rhythms, unyielding against the chaos often brought forth by humanity.

"I will protect you," Leo whispered fervently, his voice barely more than a breath, yet filled with an unyielding determination. As the resolution crystallized within his heart, it became more than just a wish; it was a solemn promise. "I will stand by your side." This declaration marked a pivotal moment for Leo—a turning point that transcended the superficial chase for glory he had long harbored in his heart. In that instant, he understood that his remarkable gift, the extraordinary abilities that set him apart, were not meant for selfish ambition but rather for fostering deep connections and embodying a sense of guardianship over the natural world. He would not wield his powers to bend the ocean to his will, coercing it into submission; instead, he would harness them to amplify its voice, acting as a bridge between humanity and the hidden depths of nature, echoing its needs and cries to the world above. His purpose crystallized into a beacon for others—a champion who would light the path toward respect and reverence for the wondrous ocean.

With this newfound clarity and determination coursing through his veins, igniting a fire of passion within him, Leo took one last, lingering glance at the majestic landscape spread out before him. The rugged cliffs and crashing waves formed a breathtaking panorama—a view that would forever be etched in his memory. Slowly, he turned away from the precipice, redirecting his focus toward a future brimming with possibility. Leo understood that he must gather the wisdom he had acquired, seeking out kindred spirits who shared his vision for the ocean's protection. Together, they would embark on a transformative journey, one that would lead them to become true stewards of the seas. He envisioned vibrant campaigns and educational initiatives designed to champion the safeguarding of fragile marine habitats, to enlighten the public about the delicate interconnection of these ecosystems, and to inspire a collective effort to restore what had been lost to years of neglect and exploitation.

As Leo stepped back from the cliff's edge, he felt the ocean's presence enveloping him—not as a master to be controlled, but as a mighty ally, encouraging him to embrace his commitment. His heart soared with the same energy that pulsed tirelessly through the tides—strong, unwavering, and resolute. In the depths of his being, he made a silent vow, a promise etched deep within his soul: he would always respect and protect these waters, nurturing the vital relationship that bound him to the wondrous sea for all time. No sacrifice would be too great, no challenge too daunting; he would dedicate himself wholly to this sacred trust.

The path that lay ahead would not be easy; it was destined to be fraught with formidable challenges and intense confrontations from those who sought to exploit the ocean's precious resources for their selfish ambitions. He knew well that greed would rear its ugly head in many forms, and that countless individuals and corporations would stop at nothing to plunder the depths of the sea for treasure and gain. Yet, in Leo's heart, a fierce conviction burned brightly. He felt an undeniable sense of purpose swelling within him. What greater cause could there be than the unwavering defense of the sacred realms that lay beneath the waves, teeming with life and mystery? This mission was not merely about protecting the ocean; it was about safeguarding the delicate balance of nature itself, an endeavor that resonated deeply with his very being. Leo vowed to rise against these challenges head-on, unyielding in the face of opposition, determined to let his actions echo through the world he sought to defend.

With one last heartfelt glance at the horizon, where the endless expanse of the sea met the vast sky in a harmonious embrace, Leo began his journey back toward the village—a place he had known all his life, yet felt new and different now. He was not just a young man blessed with extraordinary powers; he had transformed into a protector of the deep—a guardian of the living sea. Each step he took down the rocky path felt imbued with purpose and resolve, a quiet acknowledgment that he was answering a call that transcended his own desires, a call to something far greater than himself. It was as if the very water around him was whispering encouragement, sending him forth with its ethereal blessing. Each wave that lapped eagerly at the shore served as a poignant reminder of the mission he had accepted, each splash reaffirming his commitment.

As Leo descended, he felt an uplifting energy coursing through him, invigorating him for the trials that lay ahead. It felt as though the ocean itself was empowering him, infusing him with strength for the challenges to come. The weight of doubt that had once burdened his spirit gradually lifted, replaced by a newfound sense of clarity and determination. He understood now that no storm, no matter how tempestuous, could sway him from his course or deter him from his mission. Where he had once felt uncertainty, a steady resolve now pulsed through his veins. He was ready, now more than ever, to face the tumultuous storms ahead—both those raging within the hearts of men, wrought by ambition and greed, and those brewing in the unpredictably wild ocean, fierce and unyielding. With a heart full of resolve and a spirit unbreakable, Leo embraced his destiny, prepared to stand as an unwavering bulwark against those who would dare to challenge the sanctity of the sea, determined to defend the irreplaceable treasures that lay beneath the surface of the waves.

Chapter 15

The path that lay ahead would not be easy; it was destined to be fraught with formidable challenges and intense confrontations from those who sought to exploit the ocean's precious resources for their selfish ambitions. Greed would inevitably rear its ugly head, and Leo was acutely aware that many would stop at nothing to plunder the depths of the sea for treasure and gain, viewing the vast aquatic realm merely as a bounty to be harvested. This insatiable greed, like a shadow creeping across the sunset, threatened to overshadow not only the rich diversity of marine life but also the very balance that sustained the fragile ecosystems beneath the waves.

Yet, in the depths of Leo's heart, a fierce conviction burned brightly, illuminating his spirit with unwavering resolve. What greater cause could there be than the noble and unwavering defense of the sacred realms that lay deep beneath the ocean's surface, teeming with life and mystery yet untouched by human avarice? It was not merely about protecting the ocean itself; it was about preserving the delicate balance of nature, a mission that resonated deeply within him and guided his every thought and action. To Leo, every creature of the sea, from the tiniest plankton to the majestic whales, played a vital role in the tapestry of life that thrived beneath the waves, and he felt a profound responsibility to protect it. He could not stand idly by and watch as the treasures of the ocean became victims to ruthless exploitation.

With this dedication firmly rooted in his soul, he would rise to confront those formidable challenges head-on, undeterred by the powerful opposition that awaited him. He was determined to let his actions speak volumes, advocating for the world he sought to defend—a world where the water shimmered without fear of pollution and where the creatures of the deep swam freely, unharmed by man's greed.

As he stood at the threshold of the horizon, casting one last heartfelt glance at the expansive ocean where the endless waves met the vast sky in a perfect embrace, Leo began his journey back toward the village. He was not just a young man blessed with extraordinary powers; he had transformed into a protector of the deep—a guardian of the living sea, chosen by fate for a grand purpose. Each step he took down the rocky path felt imbued with purpose and resolve, a quiet acknowledgment that he was answering a call far greater than himself. It was as if the very water surrounding him was whispering words of encouragement, sending him forth with its ethereal blessing. Each wave lapping at the shore served as a gentle reminder of the monumental mission he had accepted, inspiring him to proceed with courage.

As Leo descended, an uplifting energy coursed through him, as if the very essence of the ocean was empowering him for the trials that lay ahead. The once heavy weight of doubt that had burdened his spirit gradually lifted, replaced instead by a clear sense of clarity and steadfast determination. He now understood that no storm, regardless of its tempestuous nature, could deter him from his chosen course. He was ready—now more than ever—to confront the tumultuous storms ahead, both those raging within the hearts of men who sought to exploit the ocean and those brewing in the unpredictably wild waters themselves. With a resolute heart and an unwavering spirit, Leo boldly embraced his destiny, prepared to stand as an unyielding bulwark against anyone who would dare to challenge the sanctity of the sea.

As the moon rose high in the starlit sky, casting a silvery sheen upon the restless waters below, Leo ventured bravely into the unforgiving embrace of the night. The ocean roared with fierce intensity, waves crashing against one another with fervor, almost as if they were sentient beings questioning his very resolve as he prepared to face the immense challenges lying ahead. In the distance, he gazed upon the once proud glory of his hometown, its silhouette gradually fading beneath a burgeoning darkened veil of night, a poignant reminder of what had been lost and what he held dear to his heart—the stubborn memory of a home that thrummed with vibrant life and laughter.

The small boat he rode rocked precariously with each tumultuous rise and fall of the relentless waves. Each heave sent a wave of trepidation coiling tightly in his stomach, like a serpent poised to strike at the slightest moment of weakness. Legends and whispered tales spoke of the Leviathan—a creature of such immense size and power that it defied imagination, lurking in the very depths he was now navigating. Its glistening scales, slick and ominous in the inky waters, glinted like jewels in the night, a constant reminder of the dangers that lurked beneath him. Its eyes, twin orbs swirling with tempestuous energy akin to stormy skies, haunted his thoughts and fueled the unsettling uncertainty gnawing at him. But as fear threatened to grip his heart, Leo reminded himself of his purpose, drawing strength from the knowledge that he stood not alone, but as part of something much larger—a living force devoted to protect the ocean and all its wonders from the ravages of greed.

Just as exhaustion threatened to engulf his mind and body, the water surrounding him began to surge and ripple violently, dark shadows swirling ominously just below the surface. Every muscle in Leo's body ached, and fatigue weighed heavily upon him like an anchor dragging him into the depths of despair. Gripping the sides of the small boat with trembling hands, he felt his heart pounding fiercely in rhythm with the relentless waves slapping against the hull. He forced himself to steady his breathing; fear and anxiety threatened to overwhelm him, but he pushed against them, summoning every ounce of resolve within him.

In his hand, he brandished his staff, a powerful relic that stood as both a symbol of hope and the catalyst for his strength. Its surface was engraved with intricate patterns, glinting with a light that seemed to resonate with the very essence of his spirit. As he stood tall on the rocking boat, he shouted defiantly into the void, projecting his voice into the dark abyss that loomed ahead, "Show yourself!" His voice rang out, buoyed by a fierce determination, echoing into the night as he prepared himself to confront the legendary creature that had long lingered in the deep, shrouded in mystery and fear.

In an instant, the very air around him seemed to pulse with uncontainable force. A massive, thunderous crash echoed through the night, reverberating across the endless expanse of the dark ocean and startling the nocturnal creatures that inhabited the shores. The Leviathan erupted from the depths, breaking the surface in a display of unimaginable power and majesty. It was a colossal beast, a living embodiment of the ocean intertwined with the elemental forces of nature itself. The water churned violently in its wake as it breached the surface, sending a cascade of waves crashing against the small boat, nearly capsizing it.

As it emerged, the moonlight illuminated its scales, which shimmered eerily like jewels—a mesmerizing mosaic of deep blues and vibrant greens that seemed to reflect the very soul of the sea. Its hunched back was lined with dorsal fins that glistened with moisture, while its elongated body twisted gracefully through the waves. The creature's eyes glowed dimly, imbued with centuries of ancient sadness and fury that reverberated with the primal forces of nature. They pierced through Leo's heart, compelling him to confront the gravity of this moment.

The air crackled with potent energy, charged with an electric ambiance that promised confrontation. Leo stood firm, feeling the ship rock violently beneath him as the Leviathan's presence enveloped him. This was no ordinary encounter; the confrontation between man and myth had begun in earnest. In that pivotal moment, he understood that this encounter would not be merely a test of strength, but rather a poignant battle of wills—a clash between unyielding hope and the sinister depths of despair—an epic struggle against the very embodiment of the ocean's wildest fury. Leo's heart raced with anticipation, fuelled by the flames of determination flickering in his chest as he braced himself to confront the unfathomable unknown.

"Why do you come here, mortal?" The Leviathan's voice boomed with an overpowering resonance, echoing through the very bones of the sea itself, creating a sound that felt like distant thunder reverberating in the air. The water around Leo surged upward, splashing violently as though responding to the primordial demand of the creature, generating ripples that spread far beyond their immediate vicinity.

"I seek to understand why you bring destruction upon my people!" Leo shouted back, his heart racing in his chest like a trapped bird desperate to escape its cage. The salty tang of ocean spray clung to his skin, invigorating and chilling him simultaneously, as he glared defiantly at the massive form of the Leviathan towering above him, casting a shadow that enveloped the small vessel. "You were once a guardian, a protector of the seas and its creatures—why have you forsaken your noble role?" His voice echoed through the turmoil, filled with desperation and a hint of fury, intertwining with the roar of the angry waves.

The Leviathan responded with a deafening roar that rippled through the water, churning it into frothy chaos. Water cascaded off its magnificent form, sparkling like diamonds scattered across the sea, drenching Leo to the bone as he braced himself against the relentless tide. "I am not the wicked one; it is the greed and hate that have stained these waters," it proclaimed, its voice layered with a mixture of contempt and sorrow. "I am bound by the chaos of mankind's making; I rise to reclaim the ocean that was once pure, a sacred realm free of the filth and despair you have brought forth."

Leo's heart sank as he absorbed the truth in the creature's words. This was no mindless beast; the Leviathan was a manifestation of the world's turmoil, a guardian twisted by the sorrow and rage that mankind had manifested upon the seas. Understanding the depth of its anguish, Leo's determination burned even brighter. "Then let us confront this darkness together. I will return the empathy of humankind to the depths—let us purify the waters and restore the balance that once existed!" he exclaimed, a surge of resolve igniting within him like a phoenix rising from its ashes.

The sea raged around them, waves crashing violently in response to the Leviathan's power, and the creature's piercing gaze locked onto Leo's, deep and ancient. He felt the weight of destiny settle upon his shoulders, and he understood that the stakes were incredibly high. His heart was burdened by the realization that success in this endeavor would require risking everything he held dear—his life, his beliefs, and his very soul. Through his own harrowing experiences, he had learned that true strength and courage often demanded a price—one that could not be easily paid.

"Very well," the beast hissed, its voice a rumbling thunder that calmed the stormy waters slightly in acknowledgment of Leo's bravery. "But know this: the sacrifice must be made. This is not an endeavor for the faint-hearted." The words hung in the air like a foreboding omen, and as the fearsome beast loomed over him, Leo felt the weight of history swelling in the waters—a tidal wave of emotions, ancient grief, and the promise of redemption. The time for change had come, and he was ready to plunge into the depths of legend, his heart forged in hope and unwavering courage.

Leo took a deep breath, his lungs filling with the brine of the ocean air, understanding the weight of its somber words. "What must be done?" he asked, his voice steady despite the turmoil within. The question lingered in the salty breeze, heavy with expectation and a sense of impending destiny.

"You must anchor your essence to the depths," the Leviathan declared, its immense form shifting like an unwieldy shadow against the currents, its eyes reflecting the vastness of the ocean itself, capturing the wisdom of untold ages. "Merge with the sea's sorrow, face its pain, and only then can we cleanse the depths of the world's grief. Only then can I regain my purpose as the true guardian of these waters, the protector I was meant to be." The Leviathan's voice rumbled deep, a chorus of thunder echoing the tumultuous relationship between humanity and nature.

A cold weight settled in Leo's chest, apprehension creeping alongside a flicker of resolve—the kind that ignited a fire in the darkest of places. To sacrifice himself for the greater good—not just of Seabrook Haven, but for every soul upon this interconnected web of life—resonated deeply within him. Images of his people flashed through his mind, the kindness of his neighbors, the laughter of children skipping stones on the shore, and the echoes of laughter now tainted by sorrow. He thought of the suffering so many had endured, their voices blending into the relentless crashing of waves against the cliffs. Still, doubt flickered briefly in his mind, like the shadows in the depths of the ocean, whispering questions that sent tremors of uncertainty through him: could he truly possess the strength to undertake such a daunting task? Could he confront a sorrow that was not his own but that of an entire world ravaged by indifference and greed?

"I shall hold the light for you," he uttered, his voice steady yet tinged with the weight of deep understanding, accepting the heavy truth that lay before him. There was a finality in his words, as though they forged a pact woven into the fabric of fate itself. In that fleeting moment, he grasped the enormity of the task ahead, a burden that loomed before him like a storm on the horizon—impossible yet undeniably necessary. As his words drifted into the heavy air surrounding them, something miraculous began to unfold. A warm, luminescent glow radiated from his very core, illuminating the dark waters that had encased them in shadow. The light danced like a thousand fireflies, casting flickering reflections across the surface, compelling the oppressive darkness to recede with resilience and grace.

As the formidable Leviathan plunged back into the abyssal depths, Leo felt an undeniable magnetic pull of the ocean beckoning him downward, as if the depths themselves were alive and yearning for his presence. There was a strange allure to the murky depths, an invitation—a siren's call he found difficult to resist. He surrendered himself to the swirling waters, allowing the ethereal current to envelop him like a comforting blanket woven from the fabric of memories—memories that echoed through his mind like a nostalgic melody: the laughter of children playing on the shore, remnants of joy mingling with the grief of lost souls, the life of the sea that thrived around him like a vibrant tapestry. In those cold, darkened depths, pain and sorrow resonated within him, each image of past struggles manifesting vividly, drawing him deeper into their haunting embrace as though the ocean itself was revealing its scars.

As the suffocating darkness began to fade under the warmth of his burgeoning spirit, a new sensation enveloped him—a strange warmth that pulsed through the water, and he could feel the heart of the ocean synchronizing with his own rhythm. It was a beating, pulsing essence that resonated through every fibre of his being, as if he had become part of something far greater than himself. The Leviathan returned, not as a foe but as an ally, coiling gently around him, its ancient bones weaving a tapestry of light, restoring what had been lost to the melancholy void of despair. In this extraordinary moment, they became a conduit—a confluence of pain and resolution, almost as if time itself had bent to their will, granting them a glimpse of salvation that transcended the bounds of existence as Leo once knew it.

In that moment of sacrifice, Leo transcended the limitations of mere humanity. He was no longer just a man navigating the tumultuous seas; he had become a guardian of the ocean—a sentinel tasked with restoring the delicate balance between light and dark. The water surged triumphantly around him, celebrating his decision, reflecting the newfound hope that radiated through the waves, a vibrant expression of life renewed. It was as if the very ocean celebrated his choice, aligning its currents into a symphony of resilience that echoed through the vast expanse.

Back in the quaint village of Seabrook Haven, the villagers gathered at the shore, captivated by the transformation taking place before their eyes. Faces turned toward the horizon, their hearts intertwined with the spectacle unfolding in the water. They watched in awe as the tumultuous ocean began to calm, its once-turbulent depths shimmering with renewed vibrancy—the colours of the sea shifting into mesmerizing hues that sparkled under the sun's golden gaze. A palpable sense of peace wafted through the salty air, resonating through every heart with comforting familiarity—an embrace that whispered of brighter days to come, a reassurance that the guardian was alive and resolute. The world felt a shift, an awakening, as if the very tide had conspired with Leo to weave a richer tapestry of hope and renewal for all who called the ocean their home.

Though Leo had seemingly vanished beneath the waves, his presence lingered on in the hearts and souls of the villagers, echoing through their memories like the soft, relentless lapping of the tide against the shore. His essence became intertwined with the very fabric of their community, a spirit infused with courage and resilience—a quiet hero whose life had been a testament to unselfish sacrifice. He had not merely existed among them; he had given everything, weaving a narrative that transformed the ordinary into the extraordinary.

As the sun began its ascent, painting the horizon in hues of gold and orange, the villagers felt a renewed sense of purpose ignite within them. The morning light would soon rise, casting its illuminating glow on the path forward. They would carry forth Leo's legend like a torch, proudly brandishing it as a symbol of hope—a bright beacon that illuminated not just their shared history, but the values they held dear. It served as a constant reminder that sometimes, true strength does not stem from sheer power or bravado. Instead, it lies in the profound willingness to give of oneself, prioritizing the greater good over personal gain.

Gathered together, united by their memories, they recounted stories of Leo's bravery, his unwavering spirit, and the promises he had fulfilled. Each tale shared served to strengthen their bond, reminding them of what Leo had stood for. In their hearts, they realized that the ocean had a guardian once more, for Leo's spirit was not lost; it was guiding them from the depths, whispering encouragement as they faced their own challenges. They felt reassured that light would always shine, even in the darkest of times, as long as they clung to the ideals he had embodied.

Leo's legacy was far more than a memory; it was a living symphony of hope and courage that would ripple through the waters for generations to come. It would flow through the veins of their community, echoing the timeless truth that from sacrifice can arise profound strength and resilience. The villagers understood that in the depths of despair, it was Leo's spirit that would continue to illuminate their way, offering warmth and light, even when the storms of life threatened to engulf them. Thus, they vowed to honor him, to live with the same selflessness and dedication that he had shown, ensuring that his memory would endure, vibrant and alive, in the hearts of all who called the village home.

Chapter 16

With a heavy heart, Leo set out on a quest that weighed heavily upon his spirit, determined to confront the insidious evil lying in wait beneath the turbulent waves. This malevolent force had infiltrated the very essence of the Celestial Sea, a once-cherished sanctuary that now bore the scars of darkness. Where the waters had once danced in tranquil beauty, they now roiled with turbulence, tainted and corrupted by a presence that threatened to consume all forms of life. The vibrant aquatic paradise that had flourished for centuries was now marred, a blight upon its natural splendor.

Standing at the precipice of a high cliff, Leo gazed down into the churning abyss below. The salty spray of the ocean kissed his face, mingling with tears that threatened to spill from his eyes—a poignant reminder of the gravity of his undertaking. In that moment, he felt the immense weight of destiny settle firmly upon his shoulders. Each crashing wave was imbued with the essence of expectations, both his own and those of every creature that called the Celestial Sea home. It was as if he could hear their cries, muffled by the crushing depths, each one a plea for a savior, a beacon of hope in the encroaching darkness.

The sky above mirrored the turmoil in his heart, crackling with volatile energy as storm clouds gathered ominously overhead like sentinels of despair. The thunderous roars that rumbled through the air echoed his conflicted thoughts, each boom a flicker of apprehension and a clarion call to resolve. With a deep breath, he closed his eyes, shutting out the chaos that surrounded him and reaching inward, delving deep into his core. He summoned the potent powers that flowed through him—an ancient connection to the very currents of the ocean, the whispers of the wind that danced through the rugged rock formations, and the warm, flickering light of determination that glimmered insistently within his heart. This was the defining moment, the pivotal intersection where he would need to lay it all on the line—both for the sea and the myriad beings that inhabited its depths.

With a resolute determination, Leo leaped into the water, the sea enveloping him like a long-lost friend, embracing him after what felt like years of separation. As he descended deeper, the chill of the water surrounded him, fueling his courage as he cast an incantation that illuminated the murky depths. A vibrant, thriving underwater world unveiled itself before his eyes, bursting with life and color—a vivid reminder of all that was at stake. Schools of brightly colored fish darted about like living jewels, their scales glinting in the newfound light. Majestic corals bloomed in splendid hues, vibrant against the backdrop of the sandy ocean floor, which shimmered and danced like tiny stars beneath his movements.

But as Leo swam closer to the epicenter of the malevolent darkness that now seemed to haunt this once-pristine paradise, the beauty around him twisted into a dreadful reality. Towering above him, obscured by the depths, was a massive leviathan—a creature of legend, its scales as black as the deepest night itself, swallowing the light around it. Its eyes glowed with an unnatural, malevolent light, sending chills coursing through his veins. The creature twisted and writhed in the water, commanding the tempest swirling around it like a masterful conductor leading an orchestral chaos. Every flourish of its formidable appendages sent powerful waves crashing against the ocean floor, resonating dread and despair into the hearts of those who might witness its fury.

Though fear gripped Leo's heart with unrelenting force, it was accompanied by an unshakeable determination that ignited like a flame within him. With each powerful stroke of his arms, he propelled himself forward, drawing strength from the memories of all the lives that depended on him—the innocent creatures that deserved to thrive in harmony with the tide, who were now threatened by the leviathan's rampage. Leo could almost see their faces in his mind's eye, tender and pleading, filled with hope and urging him to push through the suffocating fear that clung to him.

As he drew closer to the leviathan, a guttural battle cry erupted from the depths of his being, reverberating through the water with an intensity that resonated against the dark reign of the creature before him. With every ounce of energy he could muster and the combined strength of his purpose, Leo unleashed waves of brilliant light and pent-up energy that cascaded through the watery domain. Each pulse was a declaration of his newfound purpose, a testament to his unyielding resolve to dispel the shadows and reclaim the sanctuary that had been lost.

The leviathan roared in response, a bellowing challenge that seemed to shake the very foundations of the ocean itself. Its thunderous voice, deep and guttural, resonated like an ominous harbinger of the storm to come, echoing across the vast expanse of water. The ocean, in reply, unleashed its fury, waves crashing fiercely upon one another, as if conjuring all elemental forces in anticipation of the cataclysmic clash between the forces of good and evil.

Standing resolute amid the swelling tide, Leo raised his arms high, invoking the ancient spirits of the sea to join him in this critical struggle. The waters around him stirred and swirled, taking on life as if they were sentient beings. Among the surging tides appeared the jellyfish of enlightenment, their translucent forms drifting gracefully, pulsing with a soothing glow. Nearby, the dolphins of joy leapt exuberantly, their playful energy infectious, while the sharks of ferocity sliced through the water with fierce determination, their sleek bodies gliding purposefully into the fray. These magnificent creatures were no mere observers; they were allies in this monumental battle against the encroaching darkness.

The clash that unfolded was tumultuous and fierce, the stakes raised higher than anyone had dared to imagine. The leviathan, sensing the resolve of its adversaries, retaliated with torrential waves of darkness, hurling currents of shadowy energy that crashed against Leo with a force that threatened to send him tumbling off balance. The immense pressure sought to smother his spirit, to suffocate his resolve, but he could not, and would not, yield—especially not now, when he stood on the very brink of a defining moment that could alter the fate of all.

With sheer grit and unwavering resilience, Leo anchored himself to the ocean floor, digging his feet into the gritty sand below. He regrounded himself in the reality he fought for—a vision of a world where life could flourish, unburdened by tyranny and fear, where the ocean would reclaim its essence as a sanctuary for all beings. With that grounding came clarity and strength.

In a synchronized motion, Leo called upon the myriad sea creatures, beseeching them to rally behind him in a display of unity and strength. In response, they surged forward, a veritable tide of determination—their collective energy transforming into an unstoppable force of nature that bent and swooped to the will of the ocean itself. Enormous whales breached the surface, their majestic forms crashing back into the water with thunderous booms that resonated through the depths, propelling them with almost supernatural force toward the looming leviathan. Schools of fish darted to and fro like silver arrows, mesmerizing in their swift movements, creating dazzling distractions that caught the monstrous creature off guard; its dark eyes blinked in confusion as it tried to comprehend the chaotic beauty unfolding around it.

With the forces of nature firmly on his side, Leo focused his intentions, feeling surges of vibrant light bubbling within him. He envisioned a world liberated from the suffocation of shadows, a domain of balance and harmony in which all beings—human and marine alike—could coexist in companionship with the very ocean that sustained them. Drawing upon every ounce of energy left within him, he unleashed a powerful wave of luminance that clashed against the shadowy depths that enveloped him. Light and darkness collided in a monumental explosion of color, illuminating the battlefield in a dazzling storm of brilliance that momentarily dispelled the chaos.

In that fleeting moment of suspended animation, silence enveloped the arena. Both opponents squared off amidst the swirling light and dark, each assessing the immense power that surged and flickered between them—a tangible force, alive and crackling with energy. This was a moment of reckoning, one that would ultimately decide the fate of the Celestial Sea.

Realizing the gravity of the situation, the leviathan recoiled in terror, its massive form shifting beneath the water's surface, scales glinting ominously as they darkened in response to the radiant light emitted by Leo. The brilliance of Leo's presence encroached upon the leviathan's territory, illuminating the abyss in a way that had not graced it for centuries. The once-omnipresent threat of the leviathan was now momentarily taken aback, sensing that it was about to confront a force unlike any it had encountered before—a force fueled by hope, unity, and the strength of countless spirits.

With determination igniting a fire deep within him, Leo summoned every ounce of strength he possessed. He released a powerful, primal cry that reverberated across the vast expanse of the ocean, resonating with the hearts of all creatures that called the sea their home. "For the ocean! For our kin!" His rallying cry surged beyond mere words; it resonated as a beacon of inspiration, igniting the spirit of camaraderie among all marine beings.

As if called forth by an ancient spell, every Sea Guardian, every spirit intricately woven into the water's depths, responded to Leo's impassioned call. Their ethereal forms darted through the currents with newfound urgency, weaving together the rich tapestry of energy that cascaded from their combined essence. The energies of the ocean converged, swirling seamlessly as they formed a magnificent sphere of luminescence that glowed brighter than any sun, more radiant than the imagination could fathom. Its unstoppable momentum carried it swiftly towards the leviathan, this was not just a manifestation of light—it was the will of countless hopes and dreams seeking peace and harmony.

When the magnificent sphere made contact with the leviathan, the impact was nothing short of cataclysmic. It echoed like thunder, reverberating across the waves and sending shockwaves spiraling outward, crashing against distant shores. Each ripple that emanated from the point of impact carried with it the essence of hope, swirling upwards in a spectacular display of vibrant lights—a mesmerizing kaleidoscope that illuminated the once-dark waters, splintering the shroud of shadows that had lingered for far too long.

The radiant energy shattered the leviathan's darkness, overwhelming it in a deafening crescendo of brightness that pulsed through the ocean like a heartbeat. Forced to confront the light, the beast reeled backwards, its fearful eyes wide with shock and confusion. The leviathan, once a steadfast symbol of overwhelming threat, now found itself retreating into the depths from whence it had emerged, overwhelmed and outmatched.

In the wake of this monumental confrontation, the ocean was left in a state of serene tranquility once more. Leo stood amidst the calming waves, his heart swelling with a sense of victory and purpose. He had not only defended the ocean but had also reestablished the bond between its creatures and the land above, ushering in a new dawn where harmony would reign—proof that light could indeed conquer darkness, and that together, they could build a world where life thrived in abundance and freedom.

As the dark shroud of night gradually dissipated, a magnificent transformation unfolded before Leo's eyes. The ocean, which had once been tumultuous and resonated with throbbing malevolence, began to reveal its serene beauty. The once-chaotic waves settled into a gentle ebb and flow, the water's surface sparkling like a thousand diamonds as sunlight filtered through the dissipating clouds. Here, in the wake of turmoil, light danced exuberantly upon the water, weaving intricate patterns that rippled outward, symbolizing hope and renewal.

Leo floated effortlessly in this tranquil setting, a serene island among the waves. A deep exhaustion weighed heavily upon him, its presence undeniable after the fierce struggle he had just endured. Yet in the same instant, a surge of triumph coursed through his veins, as powerful and overwhelming as a crashing tidal wave. It was a feeling rooted not just in survival, but in a profound sense of achievement—a feeling that echoed throughout the depths of his being.

Around him, the joyful chorus of sea creatures rose harmoniously from the once-sombre depths. Their bubbling exultations filled the air with laughter and celebration, creating a symphony of gratitude that uplifted his spirit. It was as if the ocean itself rejoiced alongside him, the vibrant souls of its inhabitants expressing their relief and happiness, their voices intertwining to form a jubilant testament to their survival and resilience.

However, amidst this uplifting atmosphere, Leo harbored a deeper understanding that swept through him like an undercurrent: this moment of victory, as euphoric as it was, signified only the beginning of an ongoing saga. He recognized, with a mix of clarity and resolution, that the battle for the tranquillity of the oceans was far from a singular event. It was, in fact, a continuous struggle—one that demanded unwavering vigilance and indomitable strength. The guardianship of this magnificent marine realm was not merely a task; it was a calling that pulsed through his very being, an eternal commitment that beckoned him into action.

With every swell of the tide, he felt the weight of this responsibility settle into his heart. It was a new beginning, a path fraught with both promise and peril, where the waters would eternally shift and change. The call to protect the ocean's delicate serenity resonated within his spirit, an echo of the deep bond he felt with the environment that surrounded him. Leo understood, in those quiet moments of reflection, that he was irrevocably intertwined with the ocean and all its inhabitants.

As rays of sunlight finally broke through the thick haze of clouds that had loomed over the day, the warm golden light streamed across the shimmering waters, reflecting and refracting like a dazzling mosaic. The vibrant colors danced across the surface, promising a fresh start and a world of possibilities just on the horizon. Emerging from the depths, Leo felt his heart swell with a newfound purpose, a resolute determination to honor the connection he had forged with the sea that had forever nurtured him. In that moment, he recognized that he was bound to the ocean's fate: its protector, its custodian.

Each wave that crashed against the shore carried with it a story yet to unfold, an ecosystem yearning to thrive—a living tapestry of life that needed his advocacy. This wasn't merely a duty; it was a privilege, a mantle he embraced with open arms, pledging to defend this precious realm against any threat that would dare to encroach upon its sanctity.

While a significant battle for serenity may have been won, Leo understood the profound truth that lay beneath the surface: this was merely the opening act of a much larger performance. The war for harmony—an intricate dance between humanity and nature, progress and preservation—had only just begun its overture. Each new day would present fresh challenges, adversaries to confront, and opportunities for advocacy that awaited him on the tide's horizon.

Leo knew he could not embark on this journey alone. The strength of his community buoyed him, a collective network of individuals who shared his vision and passion for the ocean. Together, they stood steadfast, united by a mutual resolve to forge ahead and build a sustainable future. Their mission was clear: to safeguard the oceans in all their breathtaking wonders for generations to come. As the sun bathed him in its golden rays and the ocean's rhythm pulsed steadily in his veins, Leo felt a surge of unwavering resolve. He was ready to face whatever lay ahead, fully aware that this was a perpetual struggle—an ongoing quest for balance and deep respect between mankind and the marine world, one worthy of courage, compassion, and undying commitment.

Chapter 17

A golden dawn broke over the horizon as the first rays of sunlight pierced through the dissipating mist that had cloaked the once-turbulent seas. The atmosphere was tranquil, infused with a sense of fresh beginnings and life gently awakening. The previously roaring waves, which had thrum with fury and chaos for months on end, now lulled themselves into a gentle rhythm, lapping tenderly against the sandy shores. Gone were the days of strife; the sea whispered in soothing tones, reminiscing about bravery, sacrifice, and the remarkable bond forged between man and nature—stories that came alive with each gentle crest.

It was a serene morning, the kind that felt like a tender embrace wrapping itself around the world. The air was cool yet inviting, tinged with the scent of salt and renewal, yet the atmosphere was charged with a palpable excitement—the kind that crackles in the air after a storm, a sense of freedom regained. This was not just any dawn; it was a dawn that promised renewal and hope, a chance for everything to blossom anew after the darkness had ebbed away.

Perched atop a rugged cliff, Leo stood strong, his silhouette striking against the brilliant backdrop of the awakening sky, painted with hues of orange, pink, and gold. He gazed out over the vast expanse of ocean that had transformed into his battlefield; each wave had been a foe, each crest a confrontation in this grand arena of struggle. He had fought valiantly to protect this expansive body of water, which now stretched before him like a shimmering quilt, whole and alive again. His heart swelled with a mixture of triumph and relief, a potent cocktail of emotions that had been fleeting during the harrowing days and endless nights he had spent battling a malevolent force. Visions of those intense moments flashed through his mind—his steadfast friends fighting bravely beside him, the majestic creatures of the sea that had depended on his courage, and that ominous darkness, swirling and vast, looming with the threat to consume all that they cherished.

The malevolent force had not merely disrupted the water; it had woven chaos into the very fabric of their existence, leaving behind echoes of despair and destruction. A ghastly creature born from shadows and despair, it had come to dominate the waters, twisting the natural order into something grotesque, terrifying, and nightmarish. Leo, armed only with the unyielding courage in his heart and the ancient magic bestowed upon him by his ancestors, had faced this creature in an epic battle. It was a clash that would echo through the ages, a tale to be sung about long after his time. This fight was more than just a confrontation of strength; it was a passionate struggle for hope against the overwhelming weight of despair—a fierce endeavor to restore balance to their world, to recapture the serenity that had once reigned over the seas.

"A new day, a new beginning," Leo thought, allowing the soft ocean breeze to rush past him, tousling his hair and carrying with it the gentle messages of the morning. As he gazed out at the waters, now transformed into a sparkling expanse of gold by the rising sun, he felt a stirring in his chest, a bittersweet sensation stirring his soul. The sacrifices he had made weighed heavily upon him, particularly those incurred during the final confrontation with the nightmarish creature. Faces of those he fought alongside haunted him, and he understood all too well that the journey had not come without cost. Yet, even amidst that heaviness, his resolve remained unshaken. He had offered all he was to vanquish the encroaching darkness: his will, his strength, and, undeniably, a piece of his very soul.

As Leo turned his gaze back to the rejuvenated seascape, he observed life thrumming beneath the waves once more, the sea now alive with vibrant colors and exuberant sounds that had been muted under the oppressive reign of the creature. Schools of fish darted beneath the surface, their scales glistening with iridescence, reflecting the light like scattered jewels across a fabric of blue—a dazzling display of vibrant life that twinkled joyfully. Dolphins leapt and danced through the surf, their playful antics a jubilant celebration of freedom, and in every graceful arc, they seemed to shout in delight, assuring him that harmony in the ocean had been restored. Flashes of joy erupted from their movements, conveying an unspoken agreement—the intricate balance of the ecosystem was beginning to heal.

The gentle waves lapped against the rocky cliffs, creating a soothing symphony that blended seamlessly with the vibrant life all around him. Leo took a deep breath, allowing the salt-stained air to fill his lungs as he reflected on the battles fought and the victories won. It was indeed a new day filled with possibilities, and as the sunlight bathed his body, he felt a renewed sense of purpose wash over him, determined to protect not just the ocean, but the legacy of resilience and courage that bound him forever to this enchanting place. The dawn was golden, the horizon expansive, and Leo knew that whatever challenges lay ahead, he would meet them head-on, forever a guardian of the sea and its endless wonders.

"Leo!" A familiar voice sliced through the air like a warm breeze on a crisp morning, pulling him abruptly from the depths of his reverie. Instinctively, he turned his gaze in the direction of the sound and was met with the sight of Mira, his closest ally and unwavering friend, sprinting towards him. Her face was alight with an exuberant glow, a radiant beacon of joy that seemed impossible to contain. "You did it! We did it!" she called out, her voice ringing with sheer exhilaration, the kind that can only be born from triumph and camaraderie. With a burst of energy that could rival the greatest of tides, she threw her arms around him, and for a brief, timeless moment, they stood there—two steadfast friends enveloped in the warmth of their shared victory, their hearts beating in sync with the newfound harmony that pulsed around them, a rhythm of hope and resilience.

"It feels unreal, doesn't it?" Leo responded, his voice barely above a whisper, nearly swallowed by the swell of overwhelming emotions that threatened to spill over. The enormity of their achievement—so monumental and life-altering—was beginning to sink in, the weight of it crashing over him like rolling waves. Waves of sentiment surged within him, threatening to sweep him away in their torrent. "I thought we might lose everything," he confessed, a faint tremor of vulnerability slipping through the façade of bravado he had so carefully constructed.

"We fought for it," Mira said quietly, stepping back to gaze deeply into his eyes, her expression earnest and resolute. "You fought for it. Your bravery inspired us all to be better, to give more than we ever thought possible." In her hand, she held up a small, iridescent shell, glistening like a fragment of the sea— a keepsake that bore not only beauty but also significance. "The creatures wanted you to have this, Leo. It's a symbol of their gratitude, an inextricable link to what we've collectively endured and triumphed over."

As she handed him the shell, Leo felt an exhilarating surge of connection to the journey they had traversed and all that they had overcome. Holding it, he felt the vibrancy of their victory pulse through him, a tangible reminder of not just their hardships, but of the promise lying within the beauty that would continue to flourish in the days to come. Within that shell lay not merely the gratitude of the sea but also a profound love—a testament to the strength and unity that arise when a community gathers to fight for what is right and just. As the sun began to rise, casting golden hues upon the world, he embraced the understanding that this moment was only the beginning of a much grander journey ahead. The world before him, much like the ocean, was vibrant and brimming with possibilities—a future ripe for exploration and filled with renewed hope.

Leo accepted the shell gracefully, marveling at its surface, which shimmered beautifully in the warm embrace of the sunlight. Each iridescent hue captivated him further, its allure drawing him in deeper—this was no ordinary seashell. It glimmered with the very essence of the ocean itself, whispering tales of its depths and secrets. He had never sought glory or accolades; in truth, his heart had always belonged to the vast, undulating sea, with its myriad mysteries and unfathomable depths. Yet, in that fleeting moment, as he cradled the shell in his palm, he felt an unexpected lightness wash over him—a profound relief as if the burdens of the world had lifted from his weary shoulders. The shell became more than a mere trinket; it transformed into a powerful symbol, one that encapsulated the resilience and unwavering spirit of the world he was so fiercely dedicated to protecting.

Mira stood steadfast beside him, her presence grounding him with her unwavering resolve, and soon after, the rest of their group joined them on the shore, each bearing their unique tokens of gratitude from the benevolent sea. There was Kailan, a daring spirit who had flown into the battle as ferociously as the winds themselves. His vibrant feathers were slightly ruffled yet he stood tall, radiating pride and defiance. He had fought valiantly alongside them, an embodiment of courage and strength in the face of monstrous foes that threatened to consume their world. And then, there was Old Salty, the wise sea turtle whose shell bore the marks of time and experience—each scratch a testament to the battles fought, each groove a history told. He had lovingly guided them through trials with his enchanting tales of ancient lore. With each story he imparted, he had equipped them with vital knowledge that illuminated their path and fortified their resolve to confront the encroaching darkness.

"We must remember this day," Old Salty proclaimed, his voice low and rumbling, its cadence reminiscent of the rhythmic ebb and flow of the tides. Wisdom dripped from every word as he conveyed the urgency of their shared mission. "The shadows we face today may recede, but we must ensure they never rise again. The balance of nature, delicate and intricate, must always be preserved. For it is a thread woven through the very fabric of our existence, and we hold the responsibility to guard it fiercely."

Leo nodded, feeling the weight of Old Salty's words settle deeply within him, sinking into the core of his being. He fully grasped the gravity of his responsibility. Yes, good may have triumphed over chaos and despair today, but they could not afford to grow complacent. "We will," he vowed with unwavering conviction, looking around at his friends—his family by choice—who shared this sacred mission with him. Each face reflected determination, strength, and an unwavering loyalty, solidifying their bond as guardians of the seas. "Together, we'll protect these waters and all that resides within them." At that moment, their spirits intertwined, forming an intricate tapestry of hope that united them in their steadfast commitment to safeguard the ocean and its infinite wonders for generations to come.

As the group turned their gaze back to the vast expanse of the ocean, it was as if life itself had sprung back to vibrant existence. The surface shimmered with a multitude of colors, now teeming with life and laughter, resonating with the joyful sounds of children gleefully playing on the sun-kissed shore. These were familiar faces, loved ones they had fought so fiercely to protect—their happiness stood as a testament to the strength of the bonds forged in times of trial and tribulation. The vibrant colors of life—rich blues, deep greens, and the sparkling golds of the sun-warmed water—danced across the surface like brush strokes on a lavish, masterful canvas, intertwining to create a stunning tapestry that spoke of nature's beauty. With hearts full of resolve and familiar laughter in the air, Leo and his friends stood united against the horizon, ready to embrace the promise of adventures yet to come.

In that precious moment, as Leo stood amidst his friends and allies, he felt a wave of realization wash over him—one that transcended the immediate triumph they had just celebrated. It became clear to him that the true victory they had achieved was not solely about vanquishing the dark forces that had stalked them, threatening their existence and the peaceful lives they had built. No, it was something far deeper and more profound. The essence of their success was intricately tied to the community that had rallied around him, a vibrant tapestry woven from their shared experiences and intertwined destinies.

The strength of their solidarity had been forged through collective struggles, each hardship a thread that contributed to the unbreakable unity they had nurtured amidst adversity. This spirit of togetherness reminded Leo of the wild, ever-persistent ocean—a force of nature that, while at times chaotic and tumultuous, epitomized resilience and inspiration. Each member of their group had woven themselves into the fabric of the sea's timeless narrative, transforming into champions not just in battle, but also in the greater quest to cultivate a world defined by connection, compassion, and unwavering hope. Together, they stood as guardians of a realm sacred to them, bound by an invisible thread that only grew stronger in the presence of trials.

As the sun ascended higher into the azure sky, casting radiant beams of light that bathed the coastal landscape in a warm golden glow, Leo inhaled deeply—an invigorating breath that filled his lungs with the bracing scent of the sea. The salty air embraced him, rich with the promise of new beginnings and fresh starts on the horizon. He recognized that while their battle was far from concluded, it had merely shifted in form; it had grown into something even more significant and impactful. The ocean, with its vast, unpredictable nature, would inevitably face challenges both predictable and unforeseen. Yet, as he stood there, Leo felt a profound resolve swelling within him—a steadfast courage that surged like a tide prepared to weather any storm.

At that moment, Mira's exuberant voice broke through his reverie, her enthusiastic cry of "Let's celebrate!" ringing out like a joyful anthem. Her infectious cheer rallied everyone together, and almost instantly, the air was filled with music that flowed as effortlessly as the waves rolling onto the shore. Laughter soon joined the melody, echoing against the imposing cliffs that stood as silent sentinels over the vibrant beach. The spirit of victory enveloped them like a warm embrace, lifting their hearts and binding them together in a collective sense of triumph that transcended individual accomplishments.

United by purpose and strengthened by the experiences they had shared, their hearts brimmed with hope and an unwavering resolve. They began to recount the exhilarating saga of their hard-won victory, each story a vital thread in the rich tapestry of their history—a tapestry that would ensure that their acts of bravery and perseverance would echo through time, inspiring future generations. Each tale became a cherished memory, a reminder that the forces of good, buoyed by the strength of love, determination, and sacrifice, would always find a way to triumph over the shadows that sought to engulf them. The stories they told would not only amplify their legacy but would serve as eternal beacons of inspiration for anyone who would hear them.

As the sun continued its ascent, casting a warm and invigorating glow upon the gathered friends and allies, the ocean stood as a solemn witness to their unfolding story—an eternal emblem of resilience and the indomitable spirit of humanity. It was a promise etched into the very elements of nature, that no matter how fierce the storms of life might rage, together, they could face anything, emerging stronger and more united than ever before. In this newfound understanding, Leo felt an overwhelming gratitude for the journey they had embarked upon, ready to embrace whatever lay ahead, confident that they would always confront it side by side.

Chapter 18

Leo stood at the edge of the vibrant blue horizon, a picturesque view that stretched endlessly before him. His gaze was laser-focused on the sun as it dipped low in the sky, surrendering to the night, casting a breathtaking display of colors that danced across the water like a tapestry woven by an unseen hand. The sea transformed under the fading light, shimmering in shades of radiant gold and deep orange, a spectacular artistic masterpiece crafted by nature itself, evoking awe and wonder at the sheer beauty of the world. This scene was not just a beautiful landscape; it symbolized a deeper message, a representation of his unwavering resolve and burgeoning sense of purpose.

From childhood, the ocean had called to Leo in a way that was both intoxicating and intimidating. Its vastness loomed like an enormous canvas filled with mysteries, treasures, and splendid beauty just waiting to be uncovered. Yet now, after countless experiences that shaped him and hard-won battles fought against both nature's ferocity and the doubts that lingered in the recesses of his mind, Leo felt a tremendous weight of responsibility settle firmly on his shoulders. It was as if the very essence of the ocean was imparting an urgent message, nudging him to move forward, to take action fervently and boldly.

As he stood there, entranced by the spectacle of the sunset, the busy docks of Seabrook Haven buzzed with life, teeming with energy. Fishermen shouted to one another, laughter echoing through the air as they unloaded their daily catches from the weathered boats that bobbed gently in the harbor. The salty tang of the sea filled the atmosphere, accompanied by the promising scent of fresh seafood—a bounty that the ocean offered freely. Market vendors animatedly hawked their wares, their voices intertwining in a lively chorus that echoed tales of the day's offerings. Yet amidst this spirited atmosphere, Leo was consumed by thoughts of the monumental journey he was about to undertake—one that promised to be unlike any he had embarked upon before.

Throughout the years, his various adventures had endowed him with a wealth of knowledge about the ocean's breathtaking beauty and, more importantly, its delicate fragility. Each expedition had served as a lesson, revealing the intricate web of life that thrived beneath the waves and the urgent need to protect it. Now, it was time for Leo to take this knowledge and share it with others, to awaken in them a desire to respect and cherish the ocean as he did.

In his heart, Leo understood a profound truth: a legacy is not simply defined by personal achievements or the accolades one accumulates along the way. Rather, he believed that true legacy lies in the ability to cultivate a deep and abiding respect for the natural world within others. He aspired to inspire, to spark a flame of environmental stewardship in those around him—encouraging them to recognize the wonders and significance of the ocean and to protect it passionately and fervently.

In the midst of his contemplations, a familiar voice cut through the murmur of voices and the cries of seagulls overhead, nudging him from his reverie. It was Mira, his childhood friend and a remarkably talented painter whose vibrant artworks captured the ocean in all its glory—from turbulent stormy blues to the calming hues of sunset oranges. She approached with her signature, contagious smile, her curly hair dancing like lively tendrils of seaweed caught in the gentle evening breeze. "You're doing the right thing, you know," she said, her voice brimming with encouragement.

Leo turned to face her fully, nodding appreciatively; a swell of gratitude warmed his heart at her encouraging words. "Thanks, Mira. I genuinely feel like it's time to give back to the ocean that has given us so much throughout our lives. I want to instill in others not just a sense of wonder, but also a profound duty toward protecting our oceans and the life they cradle." His voice held a conviction that resonated with the rhythmic crash of the waves against the shore, a natural orchestration that seemed to amplify his determination.

Mira considered his words thoughtfully, her brow furrowing slightly as she posed her concerns. "But how? Not everyone has the same appreciation for the ocean that you do, Leo. Some people only see it as a resource—a means to an end—rather than a living entity that deserves care and respect." Her concern was valid, and Leo could see the truth in her observation, knowing full well the challenge that lay ahead.

"True," he admitted with a thoughtful nod, contemplating the weight of her words. "But I firmly believe that if they experience the ocean for themselves—the sights, the sounds, the textures—they might just change their minds. That's why I'm planning to conduct workshops focused on sustainable fishing practices, understanding marine life, and the critical importance of maintaining the delicate balance of our ecosystem. I want them to see the ocean through my eyes; I want them to feel that urgency to protect it before it's too late." His voice rose with passion, commitment illuminating his expression, the reflections of the setting sun mirrored vividly in the shimmering water behind him, capturing the full essence of his mission.

Here, at the precipice of both the ocean and his aspirations, Leo felt invigorated by the prospect of teaching others about the treasures that lied beneath the waves while also confronting the pressing issues that threatened their existence. His heart danced in sync with the pulse of the ocean, a rhythm of hope and determination that stirred within him, propelling him toward a future where perhaps, together, they could safeguard the beauty of the seas for generations to come.

As they spoke, the two friends meticulously crafted a plan that would not only engage the community but would also revolutionize the understanding of marine ecosystems among the villagers. Leo envisioned a dynamic program that shattered the mold of traditional education, which often fell into the trap of being confined to dry lectures or purely theoretical discussions. Instead, he dreamed of a vibrant initiative that would breathe life into learning through a series of interactive sessions. These would actively engage villagers, making them participants in their own education through hands-on experiences that they would remember for a lifetime.

His goal was both ambitious and transformative; Leo wasn't merely seeking to inform, but rather to immerse each villager in the splendor of the ocean, allowing them to witness its majesty firsthand. With every village he planned to visit, he would orchestrate opportunities for the villagers to dive into the crystal-clear waters, where they would marvel at the vibrant coral reefs that painted the underwater landscape, each hue a testament to the ocean's biodiversity. In those rich waters, they would encounter the myriad of creatures that called this underwater paradise their home—playful dolphins, graceful sea turtles, and schools of colorful fish darting in and out of the coral.

Every experience would serve as a bridge, forging a connection between the villagers' day-to-day lives and the health of the ocean that lay at their doorstep. Leo envisioned that through these encounters, participants would gradually reshape their perspectives, moving from routine indifference to a profound understanding and appreciation of their natural surroundings.

His first stop would be the quaint village of Seabrook Haven, a picturesque settlement known for its rich fishing traditions that had been passed down through generations like treasured heirlooms. The villagers relied heavily on the ocean for their survival; it provided their livelihood and sustenance. Yet, in their daily routines, they often remained blissfully unaware of how their practices unwittingly impacted the delicate marine ecosystems and the intricate balance of life that existed beneath the waves.

As Leo contemplated the immense work that lay ahead of him, he knew he was facing a formidable challenge. He realized that altering long-standing habits and traditions wouldn't occur overnight, and he had no illusions about the difficulty that accompanied his mission. The deep-rooted cultural practices, intertwined with generations of history, would prove resistant to change. However, he was resolute; his heart was driven by a passion that burned brighter than the setting sun behind him, casting a golden glow over the horizon. This flame of determination refused to let the enormity of the task deter him.

For Leo, this journey was not merely about teaching; it was an extraordinary opportunity to rekindle a connection to the ocean he loved so dearly. He recognized this as a chance to awaken in others a spark of appreciation for the vibrant marine world, fostering a growing desire to protect the very essence of life that spanned beyond the horizon. This was about cultivating stewards of the ocean, individuals who would carry forward a message that resonated deeply with the rhythm of the waves, ensuring that the beauty and health of the ocean would be cherished for generations to come. With this vision in mind, Leo felt a renewed sense of hope and possibility, ready to embark on the journey that awaited him at Seabrook Haven and beyond.

As Leo arrived on the familiar shores of Seabrook Haven, he was greeted by the warm, salty wind that brushed against his skin, enveloping him in a comforting embrace that felt like a long-awaited reunion. This breeze carried with it an enticing medley of scents, a pungent mixture of brine and adventure that seemed to whisper promises of discovery just waiting to be unveiled. The village thrummed with life and energy; fishermen moved busily about, their hands expertly preparing their colorful boats, each vessel a vibrant splash of reds, blues, and yellows that contrasted beautifully against the deep, endless blue of the sea. The lively laughter of these seasoned seafarers intertwined harmoniously with the raucous cries of seagulls soaring overhead, creating a symphony of sounds that spoke to the very heart of this close-knit community where stories were traded as easily as fish.

As Leo strolled towards the gathering place, an electric excitement coursed through him, building and surging with each step he took—an exhilarating thrill that not only filled his spirit but pulsed through the very air around him. He was on his way to meet with the village elders, a revered group of weathered men and women who had devoted their lives to sailing the waves and understanding the sea's unpredictable temperament. These individuals were reservoirs of rich experiences and captivating stories; their eyes sparkled with hard-earned wisdom, reflecting the many storms they had weathered—both literal and metaphorical. Yet, Leo sensed an urgent need for a fresh perspective, an awareness of the ocean's hidden vulnerabilities that these seasoned guardians of the shore often overlooked.

As he approached, Elder Ren, with his resonant and deep voice reminiscent of ancient sea drums, looked up from his task. "Leo, what brings you back?" he inquired with a twinkle of recognition in his kind eyes, eyes that held the warmth of sunlit waters and shadows of past tempests.

"I've come to talk about our relationship with the ocean," Leo replied, locking eyes with Elder Ren. He felt a swell of determination as he continued, "We need to learn to respect its boundaries, to give back what we take from it, and to live in harmony with it rather than as conquerors. It's crucial that we evolve in our understanding of this magnificent body of water."

The weight of his words hung in the air between them, heavy with both promise and urgency. Leo recognized that he was undertaking an immense task—one that called for not only contemplation but concrete action. The ocean had always been a sanctuary for him—a place of solace where he had joyfully explored and discovered wonders untold. Now, he felt an irresistible pull to transform that singular, deeply personal connection into a collective consciousness among his fellow villagers. He yearned to inspire a sense of responsibility and a shared love of the ocean that could lead to a sustainable future for his community, a legacy for generations yet to come.

Ren stroked his beard thoughtfully, deep lines etched into his weathered face telling a story of a life spent in close communion with the sea. "Many in the village won't want to hear it," he remarked, concern deepening the furrows of his brow as he continued. "We've fished these waters for decades. The fish are plentiful, or at least that's what we've always believed. Why change what's worked for so long?"

Standing beside Ren, Leo inhaled deeply, gathering his thoughts before responding, determination honing his voice like the edge of a sharpened blade. "But they aren't," he asserted firmly, a calm urgency threading through his tone. "The catch has been dwindling for years. Just look at the struggle to fill our nets these days. I want to show you that we can fish respectfully and sustainably. It's not just about today's haul; it's about the future of our community and the health of the waters we depend on. Together, we can make a much greater impact."

A heavy silence enveloped them, settling like a thick fog over the coast as the weight of Leo's earnest words sank in. The elders exchanged skeptical glances steeped in years of tradition and unyielding belief in the past ways. Yet, Leo's fervor, his palpable passion for the ocean, began to kindle curiosity in their hearts. After much deliberation, considering the pros and cons of his ideas, the elders finally agreed to explore a series of workshops aimed at educating and empowering the fishing community, encouraging them to adopt more sustainable practices in their ways of life.

News of Leo's vision spread rapidly through the close-knit circles of the Seabrook Haven fishing community. Whispers danced in the air, igniting excitement and intrigue among villagers of all ages. The following day, families flocked to the sandy shores, their faces animated with curiosity and hope, eager to witness what Leo had to unveil about their beloved ocean.

Gathering the villagers in a purposeful semicircle on the beach, the salty breeze tangled through their hair, the ocean's roar providing a dramatic backdrop to this momentous occasion. Leo stood tall and confident, ready to make a memorable impact. He began weaving enchanting stories—tales rich with the ocean's magic yet laced with an underlying message of fragility. His voice rang out passionately as he spoke about the delicate balance of life beneath the waves. With words as his brush, he painted vivid images in the minds of those who listened, each story igniting the flicker of imagination.

He recounted thrilling anecdotes of swimming alongside graceful dolphins that danced in the sunlight, their playful antics bringing laughter and joy. He spoke of majestic sea turtles gliding effortlessly through crystal-clear waters, their timeless journeys a testament to the ocean's wonders. And he narrated the vibrant coral ecosystems, alive with color and movement, each coral polyps a testament to delicate life at work.

With each tale, he rekindled the villagers' sense of wonder towards the ocean they so dearly revered. He described the ocean not merely as a provider but as a living entity worthy of their respect and care. Through Leo's stories, the villagers began to see the depths of their relationship with the sea in a new, enlightened light—one that called for guardianship rather than ownership, one that urged them to stand as stewards of the ocean rather than its conquerors. The gathering was a turning point, a moment where passion met purpose, and the seeds of change began to take root.

As Leo stood before the gathered crowd, he felt the weight of their anticipation. The place was alive with a palpable energy, a synergy that seemed to pulse with the tides. With an air of authority and passion, he began to share his vision, highlighting the astonishing majesty of whales soaring through the depths of the ocean. These magnificent creatures glided effortlessly, as though they owned the vast, cerulean expanse that stretched endlessly before them. Their immense bodies cut through the water with an elegance that belied their size, leaving ripples in their wake that danced playfully across the ocean's surface.

In stark contrast, playful otters captivated the audience as they frolicked in the waves, tumbling and sliding, their joyous exuberance painting a vivid picture of life and energy. Their antics brought smiles to the faces of onlookers, igniting a sense of wonder and connection to the natural world. As Leo spoke with passion, he could feel an undeniable spark igniting in the hearts of those present. It was an awakening, a flicker of understanding that resonated deeply within them; he was not just sharing information, but inspiring a movement, a shared commitment to something far greater than their individual pursuits.

As the words flowed from his lips, he observed families exchanging glances, their expressions a mix of astonishment and contemplation. Their eyes widened as they began to grasp the enormity of what Leo was proposing. He could sense that the realization was palpable; they were not merely fishers, casting nets into the water for personal gain. Rather, they were stewards of a bountiful sea, custodians of an intricate web of life that connected them to the ocean and to each other in profound ways.

To make his vision tangible, Leo skillfully shifted gears, passionately demonstrating his innovative fishing techniques designed with sustainability in mind. He unveiled a carefully crafted net, its design distinctive, marked by wide openings that seemed to challenge the conventions of traditional fishing practices. "This net allows the young fish to slip through safely," he explained, lifting the net high above his head, letting sunlight catch its fibers and spark interest in the crowd. "It ensures that we only catch the larger, more mature ones." The audience leaned in closer, captivated by Leo's enthusiasm and the clear, compelling message he was delivering. He held up the net proudly, feeling the weight of its potential in his hands as he continued, "Every fish you do not catch now means dozens more later. Imagine what our waters would look like in just a few years if we leave some behind to grow."

As he painted vivid images of the thriving, sustainable future that lay before them, a ripple of excitement began to spread among the villagers. The possibilities he articulated bloomed in their minds like vibrant coral reefs, each story a brushstroke on the canvas of their collective imagination. They began to envision a future where the bounty of the sea flourished once again—a future where their children could inherit not just the age-old traditions of fishing but a thriving, vibrant ocean rich with life and resources. Leo's vision of a sustainable future began to take root within their hearts and minds, as the community slowly recognized that their fates were intertwined with the rhythms of the sea. Each step they took in collaboration would resonate through the generations, and together, they possessed the power to help restore the natural balance that had been disrupted for far too long.

As the villagers focused intently on Leo, he skillfully demonstrated the intricate fishing technique he had developed, each of his movements calculated and deliberate, filled with purpose. He was not merely asking them to abandon their past, but inviting them to join him on a journey toward a mindful approach to fishing—a journey that promised myriad gains for all. His message was resolute yet simple: a full ocean meant a full net over time, and the future held boundless potential for those willing to listen and learn. The sun cast a warm, golden glow over their eager faces, illuminating the curiosity and anticipation etched upon each countenance, creating an atmosphere thick with hope and possibility. Nearby, children clapped enthusiastically, drawn in by his infectious enthusiasm and the promise of a more abundant future.

As the days turned into weeks, a transformative journey began to weave itself into the very fabric of life in Seabrook Haven. Leo witnessed the tangible progress unfold before his eyes as the villagers, who had once been entrenched in traditional fishing methods, began to adopt the sustainable practices he had introduced. They embraced change, inspired by the visible results of their collective efforts, their fishing nets—once seen as relics of the past—now reimagined as tools of responsible stewardship. This marked a significant shift not only in fishing techniques but in the very mindset of the community, as they began to see themselves as caretakers of the ocean.

Evenings became cherished moments as parents gathered their children around warm fires, spinning tales of ancient ocean guardians—marvelous, mythical creatures that roamed the depths, protecting the delicate balance of marine life. They emphasized the importance of respecting and safeguarding their cherished marine environment, nurturing a new generation of ocean protectors who would carry the torch forward with pride and responsibility.

Word of the remarkable transformations in Seabrook Haven spread quickly, igniting interest like wildfire and drawing attention from leaders in neighboring villages. These visitors approached Leo with a blend of curiosity and admiration, eager to learn from the positive shift that had taken root in the community. "Would you share your message with us, too?" they inquired, their voices bubbling with genuine enthusiasm, keen to absorb the wisdom and insights that had led to such a monumental change. In that pivotal moment, Leo realized that his dream of sustainable fishing practices was no longer confined to his singular vision; it had the potential to ripple outward, inspiring a broader movement that could ultimately safeguard the oceans for generations to come. Together, they could weave a rich tapestry of transformation, creating a harmonious rhythm between the sea and the aspirations of those who depended on it, ensuring that both fish and fisher could thrive in a vibrant, sustainable future.

Overwhelmed with gratitude, Leo found himself reflecting on the incredible journey he had embarked upon. His mission, initially born from a singular desire to make a difference, was now gaining momentum in ways he had never anticipated. What started as a personal commitment to environmental advocacy had blossomed into a collective movement, inspiring communities to rethink their relationship with the ocean. With each village he visited, the ripple effect of his efforts began to grow, spreading the ideals of sustainability and community engagement far beyond their origins, reaching hearts and minds he had only dreamed of touching. He had transformed into a beacon of hope and knowledge, embodying the essence of a keeper of the ocean's legacy—an identity that came with both honor and responsibility. Leo understood the weight of this role; he was not just an advocate but a guardian of the deep blue, committed to nurturing and protecting the environment for future generations.

As he traversed the coast, moving from one quaint village to the next, Leo inspired local fishermen to reframe their identities. He encouraged them to look beyond their traditional roles, to see the potential within themselves as stewards of the sea. No longer did they view themselves merely as harvesters of the ocean's bounty; they began to see their crucial mission—to preserve and protect the ocean's abundant gifts. The passion Leo ignited was palpable, sparking a transformation that resonated deeply within these communities. Local fishermen started to embrace the idea that their livelihoods were directly linked to the health of the marine ecosystem. This profound shift in perspective began to permeate the fabric of their daily lives, altering not just their relationship with the sea, but also strengthening their bonds with one another.

In this awakening, children began to be swept away by dreams of futures intertwined with a profound love for their ocean. They were no longer passive observers of their coastal surroundings; their imaginations took flight, envisioning themselves not just as inhabitants of their villages but as champions of the marine world. They pictured bold adventures ahead—embarking on journeys filled with stewardship, innovation, and a deeper connection to the waters that sustained their communities. The visions they conjured were vibrant and hopeful, sparkling with waves of possibility, which instilled a renewed sense of purpose for a healthier, more vibrant ocean for generations to come.

However, Leo had a keen understanding that transforming the heart and soul of a community involved much more than individual efforts; it required a collective mobilization. His experience taught him that true change could only arise from the community itself, organically fostering a coalition committed to both safeguarding and celebrating the ocean that had always been the heartbeat of their existence. Inspired by this vision, Leo embarked on a bold project: organizing an ocean festival designed to rally the villages and bring them together in joyous solidarity, a vibrant gathering that would unite them under the common purpose of protecting their shared home.

This festival would transcend mere celebration; it would be a dynamic platform where the rich tapestry of their traditions could be intricately woven together. Families and friends would gather, not only to share stories, showcase art, and sing songs that honored their heritage but also to engage in earnest discussions about the critical conservation efforts required to safeguard their precious marine environment. It would be a place of learning, awareness, and connection, where knowledge could be exchanged and ideas could flourish. The festival would serve as an expression of their shared love and commitment to the sea—a joyful embodiment of their collective aspirations and dreams for the future.

As the date of the festival drew closer, an electric excitement began to fill the air, reflecting the very energy of the ocean they cherished. Throughout the streets, colorful banners adorned with local artistry fluttered in the gentle breeze, each one a dazzling display of creativity and community pride. Local fishermen decorated their boats with intricately placed shells and vibrant decorations, showcasing their deep connection with the sea. Fishing nets, transformed into stunning artistic installations, swayed gently in the wind, their rhythmic movement echoing the laughter and joy of children playing gleefully nearby. Leo marveled at the spectacle unfolding before him, his heart swelling with pride as he witnessed his community unite in an outpouring of creativity and cooperation. Each participant contributed their unique talents, breathing life into the festival and enhancing its vibrancy. This collective energy transformed the environment into a lively oasis, rich with bright colors, the sweet sounds of laughter, and the soothing rhythm of ocean waves lapping against the shore.

On the day of the festival, villagers gathered in a sea of vibrant colors beneath the sprawling branches of a majestic banyan tree, the very heart of Seabrook Haven. As Leo stepped onto the center stage, a palpable sense of anticipation coursed through him. He scanned the audience, taking in the myriad of faces filled with hope, curiosity, and eagerness for inspiration. He understood that their shared journey towards meaningful change was just beginning, but he also realized that together, wielding their collective power, they could enact a positive influence that far surpassed any individual undertaking.

"Today, we celebrate not merely our ocean, but also the spirit of unity that it embodies," Leo declared, his voice resonating with unwavering conviction, carrying across the crowd. "Together, we can forge a legacy of respect and stewardship that will echo through the ages. Let us honor the ocean and everything it provides for us by promising to care for it with the same dedication it has shown us throughout the generations." With those words, he planted the seeds of collaboration, establishing a foundation upon which their vibrant community would stand strong, united in their love for their ocean and the life it nurtured. The spirit of the day filled everyone's hearts with a sense of purpose, igniting a passion for action that would ripple through their villages long after the festival came to a close.

As Leo stood on the makeshift stage, built of reclaimed wood and adorned with simple yet meaningful decorations that echoed themes of nature, the golden sun cast a warm, embrace-like hue over the assembled crowd. His heart swelled with a mix of anticipation and resolve as he raised his voice; the fervor in his tone seemed to reverberate through the very fabric of the gathering, creating ripples of energy that coursed among his listeners. It was not merely a speech but rather a passionate call to arms, a profound invitation to everyone present to join him in a mission that reached far beyond individual endeavors and ambitions.

With each articulate word that flowed from his lips, he deftly emphasized the critical importance of conservation and skillfully highlighted the deep, often overlooked interconnections that bind humanity to the natural world. As his message resonated, a wave of cheers erupted from the crowd, a spontaneous outpouring of courage and commitment that surged through the air like an electric current. This collective expression of enthusiasm infused the atmosphere with an undeniable vitality, transforming it into a vibrant tapestry of shared dreams and aspirations.

It was as if the very heartbeat of the audience harmonized with his passionate declarations, creating a rich symphony of hope and determination that echoed under the sun's warm embrace. In that transformative moment, Leo felt a profound sense of peace wash over him—an elusive tranquility that he had yearned for throughout his tumultuous journey. The weight of uncertainty seemed to lift, replaced by a burgeoning confidence in the incredible capabilities of those present.

Leo had ignited a fire within the hearts of everyone gathered, sparking a passionate drive for conservation and mutual respect that radiated throughout the crowd. This fervor was not destined to fizzle out like a briefly burned match; rather, it was a lasting flame, one that would illuminate the path for the actions and decisions of this newfound community in the years to come, guiding them as they navigated the complexities of environmental stewardship.

Yet, even amid the infectious joy and jubilant energy of the moment, Leo was acutely aware of the enormity of the task that lay ahead. The vast ocean, majestic and mysterious, continued to call to him—a deep, enduring whisper of duty and responsibility that seemed to echo through the salty breeze that caressed his face. He understood that his mission was not solely about inspiring enthusiasm but also about forging pathways to sustain that inspiration through concrete and meaningful actions. The call of the ocean reminded him that advocacy was a continuous journey, one that would demand unwavering commitment and resilience.

With resolve surging through him, Leo vowed to answer that call for as long as the ocean needed him, a promise that was etched deep into the very fabric of his being—a commitment his heart whispered to him daily.

As his imagination took flight, he envisioned a new legacy blossoming—one that transcended personal ambition, morphing into a collective movement rooted in love, respect, and a united commitment to conservation efforts. His gaze drifted over the mesmerizing, shimmering expanse of blue waters that lay before him, a canvas of potential and promise. From deep within, an unwavering conviction arose: he envisioned these waters enduring through time—safe, cherished, and gloriously free, untouched by the ravages of neglect and indifference that threatened their existence.

Leo knew that this vision extended far beyond his own lifetime; it was not merely about his individual actions but represented a promise to generations yet to come, an inheritance built on a foundation of responsibility and care for the Earth.

The future shimmered brightly on the horizon, an enchanting vista painted with possibilities. With his newfound allies gathered around him, invested in this shared vision, he felt a surge of empowerment invigorate his spirit. Together, they would navigate the tumultuous waves of change, steering effortlessly toward a world in which nature and humanity thrived in unison, harmoniously intertwined in a delicate balance.

The journey ahead would undoubtedly present challenges, obstacles that would make them question their resolve. However, with every cheer that echoed in his heart, Leo felt reassured in his belief that they were not alone—united by purpose and infused with an indomitable spirit of resilience, they could indeed transform their dreams into tangible reality, nurturing the bonds that would forever connect them to the land, the sea, and each other.

Chapter 19

In the tranquil village of Seabrook Haven, a hidden gem nestled gracefully between lush emerald hills that rolled gently towards the distant horizon and the vast, stretching expanse of the deep blue ocean, the evenings spun a beautiful tapestry of whispers. These whispers were filled with the echoes of old tales that seemed to dance through the air, weaving a rich narrative thread that connected generations. The townsfolk, their faces aglow in the warm, flickering light of lanterns hanging above like stars in a twilight sky, would gather around weathered tables, each piece intricately crafted from aged wood, polished by the passage of countless seasons and the myriad shared stories that lingered upon their enduring surface.

In tender and reverent tones, they spoke of one remarkable boy—Leo, affectionately known as "the boy who caught the oceans." His name transcended mere identification; it flowed effortlessly on the lips of fishermen as they mended their nets, each syllable woven intricately into the very fabric of their daily lives. It even found its way into the soothing lullabies sung to restless little ones who fought against the gentle pull of sleep, infusing the bedtime stories that lulled them into dreams with an enchanting air of magic and wonder.

Once upon a time, young Leo was simply a curious boy, embodying a spirit as boundless as the sea he adored so fervently. With his sun-kissed skin shimmering like polished shells under the golden glow of the sun, and his wind-tangled hair swaying with an energetic rhythm, reminiscent of the seaweed that danced gracefully in a current, he was a true embodiment of the coastal essence. He spent countless blissful days exploring the sprawling beaches that extended before him, collecting shells—as though they were precious treasures graciously bestowed by the ocean itself. Each washed-up piece was more than just a shell; it was a unique story, a fragment of a larger world, waiting to be discovered and lovingly cherished.

Leo had an extraordinary knack for sensing the subtle rhythms of the water, bearing a profound connection that allowed him to grasp the essence of the ocean's language. This innate gift—this rare talent to decipher the whispers and secrets hidden beneath the surface—would one fateful day lead him to stretch out his arms in an act of daring exploration. With a fearless heart and boundless curiosity, he dove into the crashing waves, embracing the watery depths with the innocence of a child and the wisdom of the tides, determined to catch not just fish or shimmering pearls, but the very essence of the ocean itself—its life, its stories, and its vibrant heart.

It was on a fateful summer's day, when the sky arched above in vibrant hues of blue and the air was thick with the intoxicating scent of salt mingling with endless possibilities, that Leo, driven by an insatiable yearning to unlock the deep secrets concealed within the vast waters before him, plunged deeply into the cerulean embrace of the sea. He sought not merely the bounty of the ocean, but something far more profound—a visceral connection and a deep understanding of the relentless and majestic heartbeat of the ocean that called to him with every crashing wave. With each stroke of his arms, every thrilling swim, and every daring dive into the depths below, Leo became increasingly adept at listening to the ocean's hidden secrets.

Meanwhile, life in the village continued its rhythmic flow, the townsfolk blissfully unaware of the extraordinary journey that their humble boy was undertaking—one that would create ripples that reached far beyond their shores. As the days turned into weeks, and weeks into months, Leo's connection with the ocean deepened, revealing layers of mystery that had long lain dormant beneath the surface.

Through trials and tribulations that tested the very essence of his spirit, Leo unveiled the myriad mysteries of the deep. He learned to interpret the graceful dance of the waves and discovered how to summon storms with nothing more than the joyful sound of his laughter. Yet amid these triumphant achievements, he felt the profound sorrow of shipwrecked souls adrift in the waters and heard the plaintive cries of oceanic creatures teetering on the brink of extinction. The more he delved into the depths of the ocean's secrets, the deeper he realized that his remarkable gift came burdened with immense responsibility—an overwhelming weight pressing heavily upon his young heart, shaping his purpose into one of stewardship rather than mere adventure.

As the years flowed by like the ever-changing tides, tales of Leo's spectacular exploits began to echo far beyond the familiar boundaries of Seabrook Haven. Stories of his adventures spread like the currents themselves, with his name swirled through the winds, traversing distant lands and reaching the ears of sailors from far-flung shores who sought his wisdom. Fishermen revered his deep understanding of the waters, while children from all corners of the world dreamed of him as a kind and gentle guardian of the seas. Leo became a wanderer, a tireless messenger speaking on behalf of the oceans he loved so dearly. He traversed the globe, imparting wisdom and teaching others about the enchanting magic of the waters, imploring everyone to tread lightly upon the delicate balance of life teeming just beneath the waves, nurturing and protecting the fragile existence that thrived in the depths.

Through his journeys, Leo became more than just a boy from Seabrook Haven; he transformed into a beacon of hope, a living testament to the sacred bond between humanity and the magnificent ocean that cradled an astonishing world of wonder. His message resonated deeply with those he encountered, instilling in them a sense of shared responsibility for the oceans and all who called it home. The legacy of "the boy who caught the oceans" flourished, reminding every heart that the sea is not just a vast body of water, but a vibrant tapestry of life woven together by stories, dreams, and an enduring connection that binds us all.

Yet, amid the myriad accolades, reverence, and genuine appreciation that enveloped him like a warm embrace, Leo remained refreshingly humble, his demeanor a testament to the purity of his character. The brightness of stars might have paled in comparison to the light that exuded from him, but for Leo, the true triumph was never found in the adulation he could amass or the applause that rippled through air whenever his name was spoken; rather, it lay deep-rooted in the profound impact he had on the hearts he could touch and the minds he could inspire with the wisdom he generously shared. Each story told about him resonated powerfully, revealing an essential truth: the ocean was not merely a vast body of water; it was a vibrant realm teeming with life, a cradle swarming with tales waiting to be discovered, cherished, and passed on. Leo's legacy spread like ripples across a tranquil pond, igniting a collective passion for conservation and instilling a deep-seated respect for nature that would endure for generations to come. It was as though he had sown seeds of stewardship in every act of care and reverence for the environment, cultivating a sense of responsibility that echoed through the hearts of all who wandered the shores he loved.

As the sun dipped gracefully below the horizon, its rays painted the sky in breathtaking hues of vivid orange and soft lavender, Leo found himself seated on the shore, contemplating life as he gazed out at the seemingly endless expanse of the sea. A sense of gratitude overwhelmed him, akin to a warm current flowing through his being, for he knew deeply that he had fulfilled his purpose. He had played an integral role in nurturing the ocean he cherished, fostering understanding, respect, and a sense of wonder for its depths and mysteries. The joyful laughter of friends resonated behind him, their voices merging and filling the air with warmth and intimacy, while local fishermen regaled their children with animated retellings of Leo's many adventures—a mesmerizing tapestry of stories brimming with excitement, wisdom, and life. The salty air was thick with camaraderie, a shared love for their home and the waters that enveloped it, weaving them together in a tapestry of memories and values that profoundly shaped their lives.

Yet, the relentless march of time continued, flowing inexorably forward like the tides that tenderly caressed the shore, a haunting reminder of life's transient nature and the beauty of every fleeting moment that demanded recognition and appreciation.

On one particularly serene evening, as the first stars began to unveil themselves in the velvety sky above, Leo approached the edge of the water, sensing that this might be the last time he would undertake such a sacred pilgrimage. The gentle waves lapped softly at his feet like a soothing balm, comforting his soul and whispering promises of eternity as they beckoned him to remember all that he had experienced. It was here, cradled within the tender embrace of the ocean, that he closed his eyes, allowing the clutter of the world to dissolve away as he felt the pulse of the earth resonate beneath him—a rhythmic heartbeat in perfect harmony with his own. "I will carry you with me," he murmured to the sea, "forever." His heartfelt words mingled with the salty breeze, a final promise forged between a boy and the ocean that would echo through the ages, a bond that transcended time and existence itself, linking his spirit to the very tides he adored.

With a deep, cleansing breath, Leo surrendered to the elements, becoming one with the wind and water in what felt like a beautifully orchestrated dance of liberation and unity. In that profound ethereal moment, he was not merely slipping away from the physical world; rather, he was merging with the very essence of the sea he had passionately captured and revered throughout his life. It was as if all the fragments of his existence—moments of joy and sorrow, struggle and triumph—were coalescing into a singular, powerful force, each cherished memory intertwining like the delicate strands of seaweed gracefully swaying beneath the surface. Within every drop of rain that gently fell upon the village he loved, through the rhythmic dance of the tides crashing against the shore, and nestled warmly within the hearts of every person who had discovered inspiration in the narrative of his journey, Leo continued to live on—an eternal presence within the embrace of the natural world, gently urging others to appreciate the breathtaking beauty surrounding them.

Thus, the boy who had once caught the oceans transformed into a legendary figure, a myth woven seamlessly into the rich tapestry of humanity's tale. His name echoed through the ages, forever engraved in the annals of history, transmuting him from merely a boy from a small, unassuming village into a resplendent beacon—a guiding light for all those brave souls irresistibly drawn to the magnetic pull of the sea. His passion inspired countless individuals to venture forth, exploring the uncharted depths of their dreams and aspirations, igniting a fervent fire within them to pursue their true calling. Yet, amidst the exuberant songs sung in his honor and the stories whispered across generations, Leo remained a figure of profound humility—a striking reminder that true legacy transcends mere fame or glory. It resided instead in the love that lingers long after one departs, in the respect we offer to the world around us, and in the shared endeavor to protect and cherish what we hold most dear.

As the last note of the night faded into the soothing embrace of silence, the ocean continued its unyielding rhythm, an enduring force of nature that forever cradled the spirit of the boy who had caught the oceans. It ensured that he would always live on, guiding all those who dared to listen—his whispers carried on the breeze, his essence embodied in the undulating waves, urging every seeker of dreams to embrace their potential, to dance with the tides, and to find solace in the tender embrace of the elements. In his transformed state, Leo became a timeless testament to the profound power of connection, love, and the indomitable spirit of adventure that lies dormant within us all. His journey encapsulated the very essence of life itself—a jubilant celebration of discovery, a passionate call to honor the beauty of our world, and an enduring reminder that, while our time on earth may be fleeting, the love and inspiration we share can ripple through time and eternity, touching countless hearts for generations yet to come.

www.ingramcontent.com/pod-product-compliance
Lightning Source LLC
Chambersburg PA
CBHW031551150726
47990CB00001B/309